# OBLIGATIONS

## BOOK TWO OF
## MURPHY'S LAWLESS

Kevin Ikenberry

Beyond Terra Press
Virginia Beach, VA

Chris Kennedy/Beyond Terra Press
2052 Bierce Dr.
Virginia Beach, VA 23454
http://chriskennedypublishing.com/

Publisher's Note: This is a work of fiction. Names, characters, places, and incidents are a product of the author's imagination. Locales and public names are sometimes used for atmospheric purposes. Any resemblance to actual people, living or dead, or to businesses, companies, events, institutions, or locales is completely coincidental.

Cover Design by J Caleb Design.

Edited by Charles E. Gannon

Ordering Information:
Quantity sales. Special discounts are available on quantity purchases by corporations, associations, and others. For details, contact the "Special Sales Department" at the address above.

Obligations/Kevin Ikenberry -- 1st ed.
ISBN: 978-1648550140

*For my girls.*

# Book Two

# Obligations

## By Kevin Ikenberry

# MISSION LOG

## UPDATE, MISSION DAY 045
## MAJOR R.Y. MURPHY, CO, RECORDING

<u>SUMMARY AO DATA, 55 TAURI B 3 (R'Bak)</u>

LOCAL YEAR: 672 SR (Date coding note: SR stands for "Since Rev." Origin of "SR" uncertain. Could refer to spaceside locals' first official recording of years (i.e.; revolutions around the local star), the political revolts that compelled the SpinDogs to leave R'Bak, or the founding of their first rotational habitat, or 'rohab.')

LOCAL DATE: Day 048 (of 369) (Time sync note: Local days are only 18 hours. Consequently, the local year of 369 days is actually only 75 percent the duration of one Earth year.

EARTH DATE: August 30, 2125 AD

<u>PREOP / STRATEGIC SITREP (approximate):</u>

Increasing competition among powers in the primary system (Jrar) may have prompted several nations on the main planet (Kulsis) to move up the timetable on exploitation of R'Bak during the imminent Searing. First mission arrived in this system (secondary star, Shex) 18 months earlier than on any previous Searing. ELINT and SIGINT both indicate that the OpFor is from Kulsis' second largest power, which has an entente/détente relationship with the greatest/oldest/traditionalist power.

Due to OpFor's early arrival at R'Bak, SpinDog and RockHounds (two different branches of the spaceside local population) had neither instituted full cessation of travel nor completed reconcealment of stationary assets. Many were compelled to go into hiding wherever they were, including various resource collection teams on the second planet, V'dyr, and one trade mission concluding business on R'Bak.

MISSION DAY UPDATES

000  Ship carrying Lost Soldiers (Dornaani hull *Olsloov*) arrives in system, scans, discovers SpinDogs on far side of local sun (Shex). Observes, decodes comms. Language is quickly identified as a devolved form of Ktor as it was spoken almost 1,400 years ago (approximation only). Despite linguistic roots, *Olsloov* command staff deems it unlikely that the SpinDogs would become aggressive or that they have had any recent contact with the Ktoran Sphere.

001  Contact made by *Olsloov* command staff. Purpose: acquire consumables.

002  No response, but Spin/Rock ships move to avoid further LoS/lascom messages. Pickets of harvesters/raiders notice movement of the previously undetected Spin/Rock craft, begin maneuvering at extremely high gee (often 2-3, sustained) to effect intercept. Terran cadre analyzes the situation; *Olsloov* selectively jams OpFor broad-comms. Only transmission completed by OpFor was decrypted as "Investigating local anomaly; stand by for details." Narrow-beam comms blocked by position of companion star (Shex), which occluded receivers located in the primary (Jrar) system.

003 Sensor results from *Olsloov* indicate that OpFor's hi-gee maneuvers are consistent with a) intercept of SpinDog craft and b) repositioning to clear transmission coordinates to Jrar. Capt. Mara Lee, USAF, is restored from cryogenic suspension to assist in battlefield support and liaison duty with SpinDog matriarchy.

004 Contact established with Spin/Rock leadership using Dornaani translation system to update language from classic Ktor and to crack cyphers. Agreement reached. Compromised Spin/Rock craft adjust course to flee toward prearranged coordinates in outer system. Intercept trajectory for OpFor intersects optimal ambush point for *Olsloov* and her drones/ROVs. Captain Lee receives partial accelerated training in local language via virtuality immersion.

006 OpFor pursuit elements ambushed by *Olsloov* at edge of outer system. Tech superiority of *Olsloov* and her deployed assets results in complete elimination of enemy hulls without loss or significant damage. In and near R'Bak orbit, Dornaani ROVs (with direct oversight from Captain Lee) assist Spin/Rock assets to eliminate small number of OpFor hulls (mostly interface transports) and sensors. Dornaani standoff drones eliminate two planetside comm arrays with potential to reach Jrar system.

007 *Olsloov* arrives on-station at R'Bak, conducts close survey for further planetside comm facilities with inter-system capability. None located. AARs generated and shared by *Olsloov* and Spin/Rock cadres.

008 Data sharing and first meetings between *Olsloov* and Spin/Rock leadership. Mutual support and joint operation agreements reached. Captain Lee is debriefed by *Olsloov* cadre and resumes accelerated language training via virtuality technology.

009 Transfer of volatiles and other consumables to *Olsloov* commences. Captain Lee completes accelerated language training.

010 Data packets for tech sharing and replication of 20th century Earth weapons and systems relayed to and declared operational by Spin/Rock automated production facilities. Examples of each system are provided from legacy examples carried aboard *Olsloov*. Legacy examples include helicopters, weapons, ammunition, simple electronics. Captain Lee commences training of first class of SpinDog rotary wing pilots.

013 Major RY Murphy restored from cryogenic suspension. Debrief commences.

014 Major Murphy debrief ends. Light company of Lost Soldiers detached for R'Bak ops is revived.

015 R'Bak ops contingent (Lost Soldiers) commences accelerated language training aboard *Olsloov*. *Olsloov* and seeded (permanent) microsat net detect upswing in movement by advanced vehicles on surface of R'Bak.

016 First planetside training sorties of SpinDog RWP pilots led by Captain Lee. Planetside movement increase is confirmed as OpFor activity. Spin/Rock intel assessment is that they are

gathering resources to secure optimum construction site for transmitter capable of reaching Jrar system.

017 Guildmother/Matriarch of leading Spin/Rock Family reported to *Olsloov* as MIA planetside on R'Bak while conducting undisclosed SAR ops in north polar extents. Capt. Lee is cleared for, and tasked to, effect recovery of Guildmother/Matriarch, attached personnel, and others requiring rescue.

018 Capt. Lee's recovery mission achieves objective while sustaining moderate casualties, but Guildmother/Matriarch had been mortally wounded prior to her arrival in AO.

019 *Olsloov* cadre, Lost Soldier CO Murphy, and SpinDog leadership agrees to conops of joint contact and recruitment mission to R'Bak. Objective: gather sufficient indigenous forces and commandeer cached Kulsis equipment to disrupt and prevent OpFor construction of dirtside inter-system comm array. Spaceside requirements articulated; assets identified. Preps begin. Construction of improvised meteoritic assault capsules commences, with limited assistance from Dornaani and contemporary Terrans. Mission leadership selected and briefed. Training commences.

021 Lost Soldier R'Bak detachment completes language training, skills assessment, physical readiness conditioning, and is officially stood up as an active unit. Designation pending.

022 *Olsloov* completes replenishment activities, prepares for departure. Training for joint mission to R'Bak concludes. Objectives and targets updated. Final briefing.

023 *Olsloov* departs.

024 Mission dropship commences op with tug boost toward R'Bak along retrograde orbital track.

028 Orbital insertion successful. Joint mission under command of Lt. Harold Tapper confirmed as maneuvering to establish contacts with Sarmatchani nomads.

036 SpinDog transport shuttles conduct high angle insertion to R'Bak north polar regions, followed by subsonic overland NOE flight to convey task force under Cpt. Hubert Moorefield to border of Hamain desert region in northern hemisphere. Cpt. Moorefield establishes and assumes command of Camp Stark

FOB, proximal to anticipated rendezvous point with Lt. H. Trapper.

045 Lt. H. Trapper's coordinates and conducts successful Sarmatchani strike against elements of J'Stull satrapy. Mission-critical Kulsian vehicle cache, along with relevant operational supplies, taken and being convoyed to elements from Camp Stark.

\* \* \* \* \*

# Chapter One

*I can't keep doing this, Bo. I love you, but you're never here. I knew you'd be away a lot with the Army and everything, but when you're home, you're not here either. I can't do it anymore. Please try to understand. Don't come looking for me.*

Bo Moorefield folded the brittle, yellowed paper carefully and slipped it inside a plastic bag. After sealing it against both time and the elements, he tucked it into the angled pocket of the uniform blouse hanging beside his creaky bunk. That Sharron had written the letter over one hundred thirty years before didn't dull the pain of that wound. Neither did the thought of her being long dead. Nothing helped. His careful romantic plans—to pick up Sharron's favorite tulips, two bottles of her favorite champagne, and surprise her at her mother's cabin on Lake Watauga in the Appalachian Mountains—never had a chance. She hadn't wanted him to come for her, and fate had stepped in to ensure she got her wish.

One moment, Bo had been in 1992, leaving Somalia on a UH-60 Blackhawk after having accused a Turkish general officer of cowardice. The next, he was waking in a sterile room next to a bored medical technician who told him that it was 2125, that he was light years from home, that there was intelligent life in the galaxy, and that some of it wanted him and the rest of humanity dead.

After awakening six weeks ago with other "lost soldiers" hijacked from various wars in the twentieth century, Bo did spend some time wondering about Sharron's reaction when she'd received the news that the Blackhawk had crashed with no sign of survivors. For a few seconds, he thought about the money she would have received from the Servicemembers' Group Life Insurance policy he'd arranged: a cool $400,000. Because divorce proceedings hadn't even started, there was little doubt she'd taken that check and smiled all the way to the bank.

*What was it Sergeant First Class Gleason had always said? Nothing moves as fast as a cavalryman's paycheck in the hands of his spouse?*

*Or was it to never, ever, let a woman fuck up your life?*

Bo snorted and rolled off the heavy, green sleeping bag and stretched before straightening his bunk. There was no one to inspect his quarters; no one would have seen him leave the bunk unmade. Still, it was a habit to make his bed and be sure that at least one thing would go right that day: finding his bed made at the end of it.

He reached down and worked the leather straps of his roughed-out tanker boots through their buckles and tightened them. They weren't his original boots, but they were reasonable facsimiles and just as comfortable to wear. In fact, almost everything seemed a bit more comfortable. For having slept over a hundred years, his body felt better than ever. But still: a hundred and fifty years and a whole life, lost in an eyeblink.

Solace came in odd places, in simple things. Familiar boots. A squared away bunk. Divorce papers he'd never have to sign. A body mysteriously devoid of the nagging injuries he'd acquired living the life of a soldier. With a sigh, he reached for his uniform blouse out of habit. As he did, his left thumb rubbed the smoothed skin where his wedding band had been just a few short weeks—and more than a hundred years—before. He winced at the realization for the hundredth time, with a similar result.

*Fuck me.*

He pushed through the flaps of the Vietnam-era tent (General Purpose, Medium) and into the calm, cool morning of the desert tableland. The storms overnight had cleared, and the sky blazed with starlight. Given the mission underway, the small forward operating base was quiet, even at 0300. He moved down the slight incline toward the headquarters tent at the center of the small, oblong compound. Concealed by alien scrub brush, the base was tucked into the shadows of a shallow, rocky bowl, surrounded by low slopes that were eerily similar to those of eastern Africa. On the other hand, the air was totally without the humidity and stench of the cities that seemed to permeate miles in every direction. At its core, the small base reminded him of the UN compound outside Mogadishu. But instead of being filled with ineffective bureaucrats playing soldier in comical uniforms, there were actual soldiers around him for the first time in years. Uprooted from their own times, each had been believed killed or missing in action. But now they found themselves being moved about as pawns in a conflict much larger than themselves. What mattered were their shared experiences—past wars and present homelessness—and the mission at hand. All they had was each other, and to survive, they would have to stand together.

While there were many nationalities represented among the Lost Soldiers—the name they'd adopted for themselves—Bo's chain of command was simple. He was a captain and Major Murphy was his CO. Given that Murphy had already had their first mission roughed out by the time Bo awakened, there had been little for him to do except to observe, learn, and deploy from a hidden spaceside facility to the surface of this planet, R'Bak. The operation was almost unthinkable, and their situation dire, even though recent events had added a few glimmers of hope.

But those glimmers were faint. The hard facts were that transportation assets were limited. The supplies of POL products—petroleum, oil, and lubricants—were critical to maintain and ration. What fuel there was went to the weapon systems first. They used trucks and other assets sparingly, if at all, to maintain stocks in case of some emergency or combat action. However, as if nature had decided to compensate for all the man-made shortages, they had plenty of local pack animals—*whinaalani*—which were able to serve in multiple roles. Bo tried not to think of them as lizards, but they looked like something out of the reptile display at the Iuka Mall back home, except about twenty times the size of their counterparts on Earth.

More precisely, the whinaalani resembled a mixture of an iguana and a Komodo dragon. From the tip of their tail to the rounded nose at the front of their triangular head, a typical whinaalani body was about three and half meters long and stood just over a meter tall at the saddle point between their four muscular legs. Wide, clawed feet gave them great traction for both climbing and digging. A long, strong tail gave them grace and balance. They'd evolved to suit peculiar weather cycles and climatic shifts and appeared to survive the periodic Searings by going far underground. They were the largest of the natural fauna observed in their area and they'd responded very well to the Lost Soldiers.

Saddling them and riding them came even easier, much to Bo's surprise. Raised on a farm in northeastern Mississippi, he'd ridden horses his entire life and discovered that the whinaalani not only took to being ridden more quickly and with less agitation than horses or mules, they seemed to enjoy carrying a rider on their strong backs. Still, without Bo's accidental discovery of their other abilities, the whinnies would have been nothing more than a work-around for their transportation shortages, rather than an increasingly vital part of his unit's table of organization and equipment.

A herd of wild whinaalani always seemed to be near them. While they seemed every bit as disinterested in Bo's indigenous allies as the whinnies already broken to the yoke, the untamed ones were genuinely curious about the Lost Soldiers. They often followed dismounted patrols at a distance and occasionally ran alongside any of the vehicles out for their short, routine maintenance rides.

So when one of them followed Bo on a scouting hike a month before, he'd not given it much thought. He'd started hiking to clear his mind and try to make peace with Sharron for her decision, but before long, his interest had shifted to assessing the available supply of water. With the Sear approaching and ambient temperatures rising, the nearby lakes and streams were already starting to shrink and recede. He'd tried to locate signs of an aquifer or some persistent, potable water, but Murphy's orders were not to leave an area five kilometers from the base without security. Carrying a weapon wasn't enough. There was far too much about their surrounding environment they didn't know.

Bo had climbed a rocky embankment to peer across the waves of rolling terrain to the south and west of the base. Near the top of the exposed stone, a flash of movement caught his eye and he'd recoiled. His mind told him it was an angry snake, and Bo raced down the rocks, not expecting the slithering black and green thing to chase him at a frightening speed. He looked over his shoulder, saw the creature racing toward him with a single bright white fang glinting in the sunlight—and ran into the leathery hide of a whinnie. It looked at him curiously and Bo's mind raced to figure out why it seemed different, until he realized the whinnie had knelt.

*Knelt.*

He'd scrambled onto the back of the whinaalani as the slithering thing closed to strike. Bo kicked a leg over the whinnie's back as naturally as he'd done on a horse. The whinnie pivoted, let out a throaty cry, and stomped down with one rear leg repeatedly until the snakelike thing lay trampled in the sandy ground.

"Holy shit," Bo had sighed as he patted the whinnie's neck. It seemed natural, and the whinaalani seemed to like it. When the whinnie didn't buck him off, Bo rode bareback for nearly two hours before heading home. He'd ridden into the compound that day to the shocked stares of his compadres.

He got a similar, if more understated reaction, from Murphy during his brief uplink later that day. The major replied to Bo's report with an unexpected, albeit thin, smile. "Seems like we've found something for you to do, Captain Moorefield," Murphy had said. They identified a half-dozen of the Lost Soldiers with experience on horseback and found them mounts. One moment, Bo had nothing but daily hikes to clear his mind, and the next he had a squad of mounted soldiers. His very own cavalry.

The whinaalani enabled longer searches for water sources and the local medicinal flora Murphy identified as a commander's critical intelligence requirement. They hadn't located any of the pharma plants, but they did come across several potable springs in the desiccating landscape as their search area widened. As the Sear approached, having a constant, reliable source of water morphed from a want to a critical need. Water, though, was only one of the unit's problems.

Bo glanced up at the clear night sky as he walked and tried to remember where Murphy told them to look for Earth. Nothing about the sky seemed correct. He knew it was a product of distance and perspective, but it made his mind swim in confusion.

*You always said you would be there for me, Bo. But you were there for the Army instead.*

Jaw clenched, Bo looked down at his feet as he made his way to the headquarters area. There was movement in the darkness off to his right and he turned that way to see a whinnie watching him intently. He smiled.

"Hey, Scout. Hey, boy."

The whinnie padded toward him, strangely silent for something so large. Scout was the largest of the males in the herd which had now attached itself to the Lost Soldiers. As with terrestrial fauna, the female whinnies were slightly smaller, but no less exceptional. Most of his riders rode female mounts because each herd resembled a pride of lions with many females and only a few males. Bo reached up and patted its warm neck affectionately and smelled the big animal's unique scent, like a slightly sweeter version of a burning tire. The odor never ceased to take his mind back to Somalia for a brief moment before he shook away the past. Except when he could not.

"Always taking care of me, huh?" He ran a hand over the warm, rough skin.

They stood there for a moment, and Bo felt an immense sense of pride and love for the big animal. From their appearance, he'd assumed them to be a reptile, but they were warm-blooded and exceptionally intelligent.

Bo patted the whinnie's neck again. "Get some rest, big guy. We'll ride this morning."

Scout made a sound that was something between a purr and a growl and silently walked away. While he always enjoyed the company of friends, Bo felt better about being marooned in this perilous future because of his mount. He couldn't explain it to anyone who'd never owned a horse, but those who had understood. The bond was something unspoken and true.

He looked up into the strange, clear sky and drew a long, deep breath of the cool air to clear his mind. He looked forward to the daily mounted patrols, and the whinnies seemed to enjoy the exercise, too. This morning would be different. With a mission against hostile R'Baku forces to the north underway, his commander's plan to lure them out relied not only on his mounted cavalry, but on Bo himself. He wanted to think he was ready.

Bo walked down the gentle slope toward the headquarters enclosure. There were soft red lights on the exterior and Bo knew the staff manning the command post would set watches outside each of the entrances. Murphy wasn't the type to let security get lax just because there appeared to be no close, imminent threat. Since he'd roused out of cold sleep, they'd been working with and sometimes against the local populations in their area. The pursuit of resources as the Searing approached presently defined life on R'Bak. The indigs' enemies on Kulsis were preparing for war while their local allies were grabbing whatever they could scavenge. Stopping them was the only prayer the Lost Soldiers had of going home.

*Home.* Bo shook his head. *What's that quote? You can't go home again?*

At the west entrance to the headquarters, the two Lost Soldiers standing guard held their rifles at the low ready. In the darkness, they appeared almost the same, and yet Bo was certain that, back in their own world and time, neither one of them had ever learned to hold a rifle at the low ready, muzzle pointed at the ground and firing hand hugging the weapon's grip tight to their stomach. Much had changed between the time when they'd been hijacked to when Bo himself was disappeared.

But some things *were* timeless. He couldn't help but smile as he heard the whispered conversation: "No. You're talking about Chicago-style pizza, man. That's called deep dish. No way. Too much bread. Give me a big New York thin crust with cheese and extra pepperoni any day. Nothing else. No salad on it. No fruit either. Cheese and pepperoni only, as the pizza gods ordained."

The other soldier grunted in a Russian accent. "Cheese and tomato sauce on cardboard is what you are describing, Devolo."

Bo chuckled as he walked around the corner. "Make mine thin crust, too, when you find it."

"Captain Moorefield." The soldier on the left drawled with a sleepy New York accent. "Good morning. See? The captain has good taste."

Bo grinned. "Devolo? You staying awake out here?"

"Too pretty a sky to fall asleep, sir. I've been telling Orlovski here all about Vietnam."

The Russian grunted. "I have listened to the same stories twice and now we argue about food. I am eager to end this watch and get some sleep."

Bo couldn't hold back the laugh in his throat. "We all agree with you, Orlovski. Just wait until he tells you about that one special prostitute in Saigon."

Orlovski turned his head to Devolo. The smaller American's face screwed up in discomfort. "You haven't told me this story, Devolo."

Devolo shook his head. "Rude, sir. Just rude."

"You're the one who shared it, Devolo." Bo glanced at his G-Shock. "Besides, I'm guessing you still have about an hour on your watch. That story should help pass the time and keep pizza off your mind."

"I am very interested now, Devolo." Orlovski nodded at Bo. "Thank you, sir. I trust Devolo does not like this story?"

"Not at all." Bo grinned. "Just try not to laugh too loud, okay?"

Bo stepped through the tent flap and into the headquarters, hearing Devolo sigh and utter the words familiar to every soldier when a great story is starting: "No shit, there I was…"

As his eyes adjusted to the red lights, Bo saw Staff Sergeant Yarbrough standing at a crude mapboard. Topographical maps were the backbone of ground operations, and while they had nothing precise regarding the ground they occupied and operated on, the renderings were good enough to show relative distance, key terrain features, and other points of interest. Next to him was a satellite communications terminal unlike anything Bo had known in his time. He was equally sure Sergeant Yarbrough had no clue what it was. The Vietnam veteran, like so many of the others in Bo's little command, had a special term for the advanced technology they used alongside their more familiar weapons and gear: PFM.

Pure fucking magic.

"Home Plate, Oscar Papa One. Negative contact. Out."

Bo heard Yarbrough sigh before the older non-commissioned officer nodded at the indig radio operator. He spoke a mixture of English and other words from a local dialect that Bo did not understand.

The indig RTO, radio telephone operator, did not reply but busily scribbled the time and message in a green, bound logbook.

"Keeping records?" Bo asked as he approached from behind the sergeant's right shoulder. "For posterity's sake or to pass the time?"

Yarbrough snorted. "A bit of both, sir. What are you doing up at this hour?"

Bo shrugged. "The usual. There's a mission underway. Even if they aren't mine, I can't sleep. You know how it is."

Yarbrough looked him over for a long moment and then turned to the map. "OP One should be tucking back in soon. The other forward observation posts haven't seen anything yet. Soon as we have comms with them, we'll update the board."

Bo studied the map. "The OPs won't see anything for a while. Even from the top of the pass, there's too much rolling terrain in the way. We could move OP One down to the bottom of the pass on the far side, but that puts them at risk if anything is out there."

The older sergeant frowned. "The real risk is if they are still out there come daylight. No matter how well planned or supported they are, something always goes wrong with night raids."

Bo didn't say a thing. He'd learned as a second lieutenant when not to say anything. There was more behind Yarbrough's comments than the sergeant let on, and while Bo suspected he knew the source of the veteran's worries, he didn't want to assume anything. Even though the sinking feeling in his own stomach said everything.

Yarbrough turned to the PFM radio set and looked at his watch. "Glass Palace should be overhead in about two minutes, now. The window will be about a hundred seconds."

Bo nodded and kept his face as straight as possible. Either Major Murphy had already signaled a desire to talk to him directly, or Staff

Sergeant Yarbrough, his operations NCO, thought it would be best for Bo and Murphy to speak at the earliest opportunity. Time to find out which. "Anything happen on their last orbit and comm check?"

Yarbrough shook his head. "The mission team talked to Lieutenant Tapper after comm check with us. Just before Tapper initiated his raid."

Bo took a deep breath. Too much could happen in ninety minutes.

A minute and a half later, the PFM radio squawked to life.

"Starkpatch, this is Glass Palace, over."

Bo had to smile. Mississippi State University, his alma mater, was located in Starkville, Mississippi. The students had a myriad of names for the quaint, quiet town that dwindled in population when the semesters ended. He'd named their forward operating base Camp Stark, for other reasons, and the radio callsign worked well and brought some daily levity to his world.

Bo picked up the microphone and pressed the transmit switch. "Glass Palace, this is Saber Six actual."

Ten seconds passed before Major Murphy's voice replied. "Bo? You're awake early. You ready for this?"

Bo brightened. "Yes, sir."

"I want you to take the mounts out ahead of your main body. Just in case Tapper's convoy runs into trouble," Murphy replied. "Once those vehicles he's grabbed have made it back up the pass and are on the way to Camp Stark, I'll feel better about covering them with ground forces and what artillery we have. It's their distance from your position I'm worried about. So I want you in the field, leaning in their direction. You can use your movement to search for water sources, but nothing that puts you out of position to provide immediate support to the convoy as it moves to the rendezvous."

"We expecting resistance? Pursuit?"

"Yes, to resistance. As for pursuit? I'm hopeful," Murphy replied with what sounded like a smile. "Once they're here, you're going to have to be ready for Phase Two."

Bo nodded. "You're poking the bear."

"Exactly. How many can you mount?"

Bo took a deep breath. "I can mount twelve, easy. There are another five or six leg infantry who are learning to ride the whinnies now. I can take them along, too."

"You can't recon and teach riding at the same time." It wasn't a statement as much as an unasked question with something behind it.

"It would slow us down a little, sure."

Murphy paused. "I want you to take Aliza Turan with you. Do you know who she is?"

Bo's stomach flopped and rolled on itself. "I do. She's one of the Israelis."

"That's her," Murphy said. As he continued, his voice was firm and direct. "She's also a trained equestrian. I know that's not the same thing as a teacher, but she's taken lessons and can keep an eye on your new riders while you keep an eye out for water."

"With respect, she ain't the kind of rider we need." Bo frowned, thinking of all the trained equestrians he'd known who were pure crap, even on simple trails. "Plus, she's a terrorist by her own admission, sir."

"She's going with you. She has asked to be involved in operations, and we need everybody in the organization supporting the mission. This is a good place to start. As for what she was doing when she was captured? Read up on your history, Bo."

"I don't think this is a good idea," Bo blurted and added a perfunctory "sir" at the end.

Murphy's voice was low and firm. "Take Miss Turan and your troops out at first light. Patrol sector four and be prepared to support the convoy as it approaches. Keep your eyes out for enemy pursuit of any kind and stay in contact with me through the relay at OP Two." Murphy paused. "Plan to recover all forces back to the FOB by dark."

Bo nodded. The mission was as clear as any he'd run in his career. "If the enemy comes after the convoy? What do you want us to do?"

"Let's cross that bridge when we get to it," Murphy said. "Find us a good watering hole if you can. Just stay ready."

"Always ready, sir."

The connection faded out, and Bo replaced the microphone on the top of the radio set. He turned to Yarbrough. "Who's your relief?"

"Lieutenant Meehan, sir. Takes over in an hour. Said he wanted to be on the comms when the recovery went down." Yarbrough didn't look happy, and it matched the return of a snarling feeling in Bo's stomach.

*Great. Just great.*

* * *

Aliza Turan woke at the first sounds of activity beyond the thin sides of the small tent. She clutched the scratchy green wool blanket to her brow, fearing the voices were finally coming for her. But…the voices she was hearing now were not those voices. Because *this* place was certainly not *that* place.

She took a deep breath, lowered the blanket, and opened her eyes. The other women were not yet awake. They were still snug in their cots and makeshift beds. Their sense of security in this strange land, and under the circumstances, amazed her. Soldiers, she understood all too well, could make anyplace their home in a matter of hours, sometimes even less. All they needed was a cot and a blanket to feel as if they were meant to be there. For Aliza, a cot, and even a blanket, were luxuries. Trust and security were not.

Fully awake, she forced herself to lay there for several minutes listening to the sounds of the morning. A mission was underway, that much they all knew, but it didn't seem to faze her counterparts. They all had their jobs to do—even the ones who spent more time getting out of their work than what it would have taken them to actually do it. The hard labor projects, particularly filling sand bags, shuffled from one soldier to the next. In her frustration at seeing men and women gleefully shrug off their tasks, she'd ultimately taken up their shovels and gotten to work. Before long, the unrelenting heat forced her to shed her familiar outer blouse and work in a short-sleeved shirt. Surprise at what that revealed gave way to guilt, and the modern soldiers eventually began to work alongside her.

*Modern* soldiers. She tossed that adjective around in her mind. They were certainly more modern than she, having been removed from battlefields in the later years of the twentieth century. But here on R'Bak, they were all antiques, long confirmed as missing and presumed dead. She snorted softly. When they told her that not only was it 2125, but that she was far from Earth, she'd laughed in their faces.

*You sound like the Nazis,* she'd said only to watch them recoil in shock. *You want us to believe whatever you tell us. To believe your lies. So you can cut into us. Experiment. Never again.* The recovery technicians blanched and covered their mouths with nervous hands as she showed them her left forearm and the blue numbers that would forever adorn her skin.

Grey-uniformed soldiers had taken her from her home, a small village named Tegernsee south of Munich, five days after her seventeenth birthday. At gunpoint, the Nazis loaded her and her family into squalid railcars and moved them toward a place she'd remembered as a vibrant city that was now only mentioned in whispers: Dachau.

Aliza fought tears remembering her parents' faces as the Nazis separated them. In the first few weeks, they saw each other often enough that the camp seemed a hardship and not a prison. But as the tide of war changed, there were fewer people in the camp from those early days. Time blurred into months and then a year. The Nazis marched her father off to the gas chamber when she was eighteen. Her mother disappeared three months after that. Her siblings…all of them in the last days, mostly to typhus.

Somehow, she was spared. Food became so scarce that, when the Americans approached the gates, Aliza and the others didn't have the strength to cheer. She saw the revulsion and horror in the soldiers' faces as they tried to help her and the others. Even as she started to heal and her strength returned, she knew she could not trust them. Free and supposedly able to return home, she couldn't bear to go back to her village and see the same people who'd given her family up on the street. She couldn't forgive them, but more importantly, she couldn't trust them. Trust would never come easily again, if at all.

Aliza opened her eyes anew and saw a few other women moving in the tent. She sat up and shrugged the blanket away. There was enough light that she could see the numbers on her arm as if to remind her she might be in the distant future, and on a planet very far from home, but she was who she was and the others, especially the soldiers, weren't to be trusted any more than necessary.

Her head snapped up at the sound of a loud, almost purring noise, and she smiled. Like her, the whinaalani were early risers. While the animals weren't horses, they were enough of an analog to settle their roles in her mind and inspire her to get out of her bunk every day. The whinnies were intelligent and docile when mounted, except for when the locals attempted to do so. Then they seemed agitated and almost angry. As she watched the creatures in the make-shift paddock, they were playful and wild. She'd grown up with horses and learned dressage from a very young age, so being around the whinaalani was comforting. And the memories they evoked, both at home before Dachau, and her life after it, were not unpleasant. Not at all.

There was a crunch of footsteps outside, and the door flap was pushed slightly, and modestly, to one side. A man, silhouetted against the compound outside, spoke softly. "Miss Turan?"

Aliza replied, "Yes?"

"Ma'am? Captain Moorefield needs to see you. As soon as you can, please?"

"I'll be right there," she said. The man ducked away from the door, pulling both flaps discreetly closed.

Since her awakening four weeks before, she had had exactly two conversations with the overall officer in charge: Major Rodger Murphy. He had taken a keen and genuine interest in her, and once she had been convinced that the improbable future was real, she met with the chief medical officer, Doctor Schoffel, to go over her medical history. When that had concluded, Major Murphy had stopped in to speak with her a second time and affirm that she had a place among the Lost Soldiers. It wasn't much, he said, but it was better than the alternative. Murphy had been kind but also very frank, evidence that he understood her from the outset. Captain Moorefield? Not so much.

Aliza dressed quickly, tugging on the boots that somehow weren't her size but didn't hurt her feet, and left the tent. Her mind drifted back to Murphy's last conversation with her. He'd asked several details about her life, especially after leaving Dachau. Where had she been? What had she done? What was her last memory? He had listened intently to the last story, even smiling at one point when there was nothing particularly happy about it. She'd asked him why he was smiling, and he'd said it would be something the Lost Soldiers could use in the very near future.

*Apparently, that near future is now.*

\* \* \* \* \*

# Chapter Two

Dawn broke in a spectacular display of purples and orange like nothing Bo had ever seen on Earth. He caught himself staring to the east, into the almost blinding beauty, and forced himself to look away. Mounted on Scout, he'd intended to move around the paddock and check on everyone—what an old brigade commander had called MBWA, or management by wandering around. In his service, especially during his time attached to the United Nations effort in Somalia, the technique had proven invaluable for seeing how work was being done. Around him, the soldiers familiar with their mounts were helping the rookies with the tack for riding whinnies. The long cold sleep hadn't affected the ability of those who had ridden on Earth, and it turned out they were solid examples and adequate teachers. They handled the job with the aplomb of old soldiers teaching the new recruits, probably what each of them had experienced in their first days wearing a uniform. In the paddock, the din of the new recruits' nervous activity contrasted with the focus and quiet resolve of the experienced riders. Combined, the feeling was electric and excitement coursed through Bo's veins in a way it never had before other mounted patrols. Until, that is, he saw Aliza Turan walk into the paddock with a bright smile on her face.

Her dark hair tied into a ponytail, Aliza wore the green olive drab fatigue pants the Vietnam veterans knew all too well. Her black, polished boots had straps instead of laces, exactly like his own. Where she'd gotten the tanker boots he didn't know; they were only supposed to be worn by those who had earned them. As fast as the thought came up, he squashed it. Nothing from that old Earth mattered anymore.

*You always said I mattered, Bo. What happened to us?*

He blinked and kept staring at Aliza Turan. Her matching green fatigue shirt was open but tied at the bottom in front, revealing a black shirt underneath. Bo clenched his jaw and nudged Scout toward her. The whinnie trotted her direction, almost happily. Turan waved to a couple of the others and stopped to talk with Sergeant First Class Whittaker. She smiled and touched his arm and the grizzled old sergeant grinned.

"Captain Moorefield," she smiled up as Bo rode up. "Good morning."

He nodded and touched the wide brim of his boonie hat. He would have preferred a more traditional cavalry Stetson, but it would have to do. "Miss Turan."

"Major Murphy asked me to join you today."

Bo pressed his tongue against the inside of his teeth for a long moment. "I'm well aware of what Major Murphy asked, ma'am."

Her smiled faded at his tone, and her dark eyes became serious. "I will assist you as needed."

"Sergeant First Class Whittaker is my NCOIC. All I need you to do is assist the newbies." He jerked his head toward a group of unsure soldiers watching others saddle and prepare to mount up.

"NCOIC," she squinted. "You mean your second in command?"

Bo frowned at her. "Yes. That's right."

"I'm sorry," she replied with a quizzical raise of her eyebrows. "This new terminology is confusing."

"Don't apologize. It's a sign of weakness," Bo said with a grunt.

"I'll try to remember that." She smiled at him and turned toward the whinnies. "You have any recommendations for my mount today?"

Bo studied the collection of whinnies in the paddock. "What can you handle?"

"They're much like horses, yes?" Turan said. "I rode dressage growing up and can handle almost anything."

"They're wilder than horses when you first get started. Not like broncos, but close," Bo said. He pointed toward a whitish-grey whinnie with a thin blaze of red along its triangular forehead. "That one. She's a solid mount. We call her Athena."

Turn nodded and followed his gaze. "She looks good. I trust your judgment."

"We're leaving in ten minutes. Let's get the newbies mounted up, Miss Turan." Bo jerked Scout toward the compound's front gate. "Sergeant Whittaker? Ten mikes. I'll meet you at the front gate. I need a SITREP from the CP."

Whittaker nodded. "I'll see that Miss Turan gets everybody in the saddle, sir. She seems to have a good handle on things."

Bo frowned. "I want to get moving. Put the newbies in the center of the formation and keep her there."

"Respectfully, sir? That woman will go wherever the hell she wants. You'll be hard pressed to stop her."

Bo sighed. "Just get them saddled up, Top."

"You want her armed?"

He thought about it for a long moment. The effort involved with taking an untrained civilian on a patrol was one problem. Providing that civilian with a loaded weapon bumped it up to another level entirely. But Murphy mandated that soldiers remaining planet-side on R'Bak had some weapons training and that they had all "qualified" at a modified weapons range built into the west side of the compound. "Did she qual?"

Whittaker grinned. "Expert on the M1911, sir. Shot thirty-nine out of forty, if memory serves me right."

"Good for her," Bo grunted. "Make sure she has a sidearm, then. Standard load. Pull extra water for everyone, too."

"You thinking it'll be a long day, sir?"

"Yeah." Bo glanced toward the high ground. "Pull a ration, too. Just to be safe."

"Done, sir," Whittaker said. He jerked his head in Turan's direction. "She'll be fine, sir."

"I'm not worried about her," Bo lied. "Have the patrol ready to move out, Top."

"You got it, sir."

As Bo turned toward the command tent and readied himself to nudge Scout into a trot, he noticed Whittaker smiling. He clenched his teeth. This clusterfuck was Murphy's idea and as much as Bo wanted to get back on the PFM and give the major a piece of his mind, he knew it wouldn't do any good. They needed more riders, and while a training program was something he and his squad could do, they couldn't do it fast enough. Not without help. He glanced back at Turan, surrounded by smiling soldiers as she taught them how to mount the whinnies from the side, like a horse. Not a man in the group was paying attention to the training as she climbed up and swung a leg over the whinnie's back in one smooth motion. Her fatigue pants were baggy, but not enough to hide her athletic figure.

*Sharron loved horses.*

*She rode dressage, too.*

Bo mentally slapped himself even before her words came into his mind.

*You always argued with me about my horses. You were never willing to hear that the Army cost us more in time and money than my horses ever did. You knew how important they were to me and that didn't matter. All that mattered was the Army.*

He nudged Scout and said to himself, "I will be glad when I don't hear your voice anymore, Sharron."

A whoop sounded from behind him. He whirled in the saddle, just in time see Turan cheering and leading the others in applause as the first of the recruits, Private First Class Boyd, vaulted into the saddle.

"Whoa, Scout." He spun the big whinnie in place and trotted over. "Miss Turan. This is not a cheerleading competition. Getting the recruits into the saddle and prepared to ride doesn't merit a celebration."

"They need confidence." She met his gaze. "And a good leader's encouragement."

Bo clenched his jaw as he felt blood rushing to his face. "Then encourage them to get their asses onto their mounts so we can move out."

Turan smiled up at him. "And what would you have me do then, Captain Moorefield?"

"Once they're mounted, I expect you to stay in line and keep your interval, Miss Turan," he replied and forced a tiny smile onto his face. "Keep the FNGs in the middle of the formation and do what I ask. Is that clear?"

"And what is an FNG? I do not understand your American love of acronyms."

Bo frowned and let out a quick sigh of frustration. "Fucking New Guys. The inexperienced riders. The ones you've been assigned to *babysit* in the hopes they can someday ride patrols without adult supervision. Can you understand that, Miss Turan?"

The mirth drained away from her face. "Perfectly."

"Sergeant Whittaker!" Bo called and looked up at the old sergeant now astride his whinnie. "Get the patrol mounted and ready to LD."

"LD?" Turan asked. There was a hint of a smile on her lips, and it nearly enraged him.

"Line of departure. As in crossing it and starting the mission sometime today," Bo growled. He turned his mount away and made for the command post.

"Yes, sir," Whittaker grunted and called for the veterans to help the newbies. Bo didn't watch. He trusted his NCOIC implicitly, but he also wanted to get an update from Major Murphy. He checked his watch again for the next communications window and frowned. The force conducting the operation should have returned to Camp Stark by dawn, and they were nowhere in sight. Bo felt a familiar knot develop in his stomach. Fourteen months with the UN, the last six of which he'd commanded convoy operations in Mogadishu, had taught him one simple lesson. Retrieving a stranded convoy was difficult enough in friendly zones. Where the enemy had a foothold? Damned near impossible.

When Bo stepped into the command post, Lieutenant David Meehan was standing before the mapboard, arms crossed and frowning. The young, dark-haired lieutenant adjusted his "birth control glasses" with their thick, myopia-correcting lenses and shook his head.

"What's the problem, Dave?" Bo asked.

Meehan turned to face him. Despite being taken by the Ktor from the jungles of Vietnam in the heat of mid-summer, every inch of him was a pasty, dough-like color. Severe acne dotted his face. Meehan had been twenty-two days into a disastrous tour when he'd fallen behind after an ambush deep in enemy territory. "Sir? Glass Palace reports the convoy is having major issues moving some of those vehicles. They are way behind schedule."

Bo nodded. "That hasn't changed from my conversation with him on their last orbit."

"Oh," Meehan's mouth worked silently for a few seconds. "It's just that Major Murphy ordered us to hold our other forces back behind the pass in case the enemy attacks."

"Again, that hasn't changed." Bo tried not to frown. Meehan was like every other second lieutenant he'd ever met, including the one he'd faced in the mirror years before. "What are you over-thinking?"

Meehan blushed. "Well, sir, logistically, we *can't* support them out there. But you've been ordered to go out there on a patrol *to* support them. Even though you're the OIC of this camp. You should be here monitoring the radio and making decisions."

Bo almost smiled. "Just because I'm out there doesn't mean that I will not be making decisions."

"But I can focus on, and handle, activities here in the rear." Meehan brightened. "Give you one less thing to think about."

*Oh, hell no.* "Negative, Dave. You are manning the CP until I return. No other duties or distractions. Not even making sure that the men are memorizing the enemy equipment manuals that the indigs passed on to us. Your job is to corral information that we'll need out there. You and Sergeant Yarbrough will oversee base activities, yes, but you will let *him* handle the priorities of work. You remember that term?"

"Vaguely." Meehan frowned. "Officers work on plans and command while the sergeants handle the business of the post?"

"Close enough." Bo grinned. They were far from any government they'd ever known, and while invigorating, it was scary, too. They were alone—to a point. "Whatever Major Murphy wants to happen will come, and it's not just us who will respond to it. We have one mission right now: to go support that patrol. I'm taking it for two reasons. One, I'm the most experienced rider in camp and using the whinnie cavalry is my idea. Nobody else can handle that. Two, the commander in the rear is almost always wrong. I'll be out front where I can see the terrain and shape the operation. That's new to you, I get it. Just because you're in the rear doesn't mean that you can take it easy. I need you monitoring the situation and keeping me informed of what the other camps and forces may do as this thing unravels."

"Unravels?" Meehan squinted behind his glasses. "You think this mission will fall apart, sir?"

"I do, Dave. That's what we have to be ready for. You're here to lead that effort. Not everyone gets to wield the sword of destiny, son," Bo drawled theatrically.

Meehan shook his head. "I have no idea what you're talking about, sir."

"Old movies, Lieutenant." Bo grinned and pushed through the tent flaps and into the morning light. "It's a fine cavalry day."

* * *

Camp Stark sat slightly back from the edge of a tableland that overlooked a five-hundred-kilometer-long valley which flowed up and into what the locals called the Hamain: the highest and most arid region on this part of R'Bak. Although well-hidden in a small basin nestled between the slopes that wrinkled the top of the shelf-like plateau, the outpost's position and altitude was optimal for providing early warning for the bulk of the aviation and heavier assets that would soon be gathering in a sheltered canyon well behind it to the east.

Five kilometers to the southwest of the camp, pushing up from the rim of the two hundred and fifty-meter-high walls of the table-land, was a small hill covered in the alien scrub. The exoflora looked eerily like sage on the western American plains but smelled entirely different. Bo had positioned one observation post atop that hill, from which observers could look down into the pass that led up to the tableland. They could also watch the termination point of a steep, dry gulch that carried occasional highland run-off south and then west to the ocean. The intermittent lakes and streams in the wide valley, like most of the water sources on the continent, were slowly receding. Where there was water near the surface, the alien vegetation seemed to be in almost constant bloom, as if trying desperately to stay alive before it died under the intense heat of the Searing.

Surveying the stark landscape from the front of the patrol as it edged downward, Bo steered Scout through a series of craters that indicated the use of heavy artillery sometime in the past. In the dust lay rusted shards of shrapnel from a massive shell, far larger than anything he'd seen used on Earth. As time and distance passed with no update from the convoy, Bo moved the patrol south of the main pass and chose to leave the rim by a narrow cut he'd seen the whinnies use.

At the top of the trail, Bo reined up Scout and moved to the side. Specialist Sublete took point and confidently coaxed his whinnie downward. Several of the newer riders went by. None of them spoke to Bo and only one dared to look up as their whinnies loped down the brush-covered trail. In the middle of the formation, Aliza Turan was coaching one of the new riders. Her eyes never left him and though she forced a smile as she spoke, Bo could sense her anger from twenty meters away.

"That's it. Now, just lean back a little and try to relax. He'll be just fine on the descent," she reassured the soldier as she nodded him onward and brought her mount, Athena, to a stop next to Scout. The whinnies glanced at each other and purred.

"Miss Turan," Bo said. He touched the brim of his boonie hat and nodded politely. "Nice day for a ride."

"Why aren't we on the north side of the pass? That area is almost entirely unexplored." She stared holes through him. "We should look there for the medicinals the indigs taught us to identify and collect."

Bo forced a smile onto his lips. "The terrain over there is much steeper than here. It would take us twice the time to descend it and four times as much to climb back up. We don't have that kind of time today."

"But those medicinals are valuable. Some of them are priceless in this culture."

"So is water, Miss Turan. That's what we're scouting for until the patrol gets back."

She scoffed. "You're not trying to find anything. You're just hoping the whinnies do it for you."

"This is a migration route for them. I'm not sure if you understand how game trails work, but they often connect to water sources." Bo looked over the passing formation again. Sergeant Whittaker and the rear element were in sight now. "You should get moving."

"Fine." She shook her head. "But I'm guessing there's no water source down there close enough for our use."

"Maybe so." Bo removed his hat and wiped his brow with his left sleeve. "But I know for a fact there're no medicinals along this side of the valley for the next ten kilometers. You can stop looking for them and keep coaching the newbies, Miss Turan."

"And you'll be doing what, exactly?"

Bo leaned forward in the saddle and nudged Scout forward. The whinnie moved as if he wanted nothing more than to get away from the woman. Bo knew how he felt. "We're meeting an indig guide at the bottom of the trail. He's taking us south, along the base of the rim. It's a path we've never ridden before that skirts the outside edge of Sector Four."

"You're taking us out of our sector? And you won't search for medicinals in a brand-new area?"

"Yes, I am. And no, I won't." Bo turned his back on her. "We've patrolled out here for three weeks now. The river valley is our best shot for a water source, even if it's an aquifer."

"Searching the same area repeatedly and expecting a different result sounds very much like insanity, Captain Moorefield." Her voice rose as she added, "Just because it's steep doesn't mean there's nothing of value out there."

Bo pointed with his right hand, "Get back in line and keep your interval."

*Damn that woman.*

* * *

Aliza clenched her jaw and pressed her tongue against the back of her front teeth to bite back a reply even as what she'd said dawned on her. For a moment, she heard Ben Mazza's voice across the dark desert north of Jerusalem.

*Just because it's steep doesn't mean there's nothing out there.*

He'd said the same words in the moments before her memory stopped, and she'd woken in this distant future and impossibly far from home.

Except she really hadn't had a home in years, not since the Nazis forced her onto the train to Dachau. After liberation, she knew that her town was not her home anymore. Germany wasn't either. The few Germans she saw soon after the Americans freed them wouldn't even look at her in their shame.

Amongst the other emaciated survivors, she'd found very few women and no one younger than herself. While the Americans nursed them back to life, she'd found Ben gnawing on an American chocolate ration bar as he sat against a low stone wall. They'd looked at each other for a few seconds before he held up the candy and waved her over. She'd sat down next to him, nibbled on the chocolate, and spoke her first words in over three months.

From there, they'd been fast friends and looked out for each other. As her color returned and her ribs disappeared back inside her skin, there'd been more than one occasion where she'd caught the attention of American soldiers only to have Ben step in front of them. One day, an American officer saw several of his men approach and circle her. He'd stepped to her side with a level of anger which surprised and shocked her. He raged at them for even thinking about her, or any of the other women in the compound, sexually. If they didn't remember that they were here as rescuers, they were no better than the Nazis. The men had averted their eyes in shame and apologized, but the officer had not let it go, swearing that he would be watching them. Every day.

That officer had worn the gold oak leaf of a major, as she learned later, but she'd never learned his name. The only other thing she remembered about him was the screaming eagle patch he wore on his shoulder. The same one that Major Murphy wore, along with the same gold oak leaf. She doubted that she could have made herself trust the men who awakened her into this strange future had she not seen those two symbols and felt the faintest pulse of trust, of safety, that they quickened in her heart.

A day after waking, she'd eaten a full breakfast and reported to a small room for an interview. There were only two chairs in the tiny space. One was empty and Major Murphy sat in the other. He'd smiled at her.

"What's your name?"

She'd told him and immediately asked, "Where am I? Where is Ben Mazza?"

Murphy shook his head. "There's no Ben Mazza here, Miss Turan."

"I was with him before…" Her words trailed off. "Am I dead?"

"What is the last memory you have?" Murphy asked quietly. "Before waking up here?"

"Ben went down the hill toward the railroad tracks." She blinked and shook her head. "He went to check the explosives."

Murphy sat a little straighter in the chair. "Explosives?"

She nodded. "We'd emplaced them on the end of a bridge."

"Why?" Murphy frowned. "Was this during the war?"

She snapped her eyes back toward his. "After."

"When? What was the date?"

"The 16th of June 1946," Aliza replied. "Our target was a railway bridge over the Nahal Kziv in Lebanon."

Murphy said nothing for a moment, instead consulting a small, glass device in his hands. "The Night of the Bridges."

Aliza shrugged. "Those were the targets, yes."

"That's what the operation was called, Miss Turan."

"We called it Operation Markolet."

Murphy shrugged. "History seems to change when the victors write it. The attack on the railway bridge was by the Palmach. Were you working with them?"

Aliza nodded. "My friend Ben Mazza and I were scouts for them. The bridge was heavily guarded, and the Palmach came under fire as they laid the explosives. We were atop a hill with rifles, providing covering fire. Ben saw something on the steep terrain below and went to check. I tried to follow him and found only a man with dark glasses. Then I woke here."

Murphy nodded again, his face straight and open. "You were fighting against the British, yes?"

"Their policies stopped Jewish immigration to Palestine. For those…like me, there was no home to return to, so we chose Palestine. When we tried to go there, the British detained us and put us into camps. It was almost as if we'd never left the Nazis, that they had simply passed us along to another captor," Aliza replied, her voice thick with emotion pent up for far too long. "All we wanted was a home."

"Well," Murphy said and placed his palms on his knees. "This is your home now, Miss Turan. You are part of what we call the Lost Soldiers."

"I'm no soldier. I will be of no use here with you."

He laughed. "And yet there you were, atop a hill providing covering fire during an insurgent combat operation. I think we'll find something you're both good at and willing to do."

And despite her silent certainty that he was wrong, within two weeks, she was putting her first saddle on a whinaalani. Working with them, first as pack animals and then as mounts brought her horsemanship skills back. She relished the opportunity to ride almost any animal, and the whinnies were agile and graceful despite their size. Teaching the soldiers to ride hadn't been easy, at first. There was a familiar gleam in some of their eyes, but like the nameless officer at Dachau, Major Murphy quickly ended any predatory ideas by ordering her trained with the M1911 pistol and allowing her to carry one at all times, if she wished. After a week on the ground, she'd eschewed doing so, especially after meeting Sergeant First Class Whittaker. The no-nonsense sergeant made sure everyone knew she was not only good at what she did, but he considered her to be one of them.

Whittaker's gruff voice shook the memories away and brought her back to the present. "Everything okay, Aliza?" Like Murphy, Whittaker wore the screaming eagle patch on his right shoulder.

She let her eyes linger on the patch for a long second before she smiled and met his eyes. "I asked the captain about our route. I'd hoped to search the high ground to the north for medicinals. Not areas where you've patrolled before."

Whittaker nodded, and there was a hint of a frown at the corner of his mouth. "There'll be time for that."

"Not today, though. Right?" She smiled, hoped that the older sergeant would reciprocate.

He did not; the radio headset attached to the shoulder of his load-bearing straps crackled to life. "Saber Nine, this is Oscar Papa Two, relay follows. Over."

Whittaker grabbed the headset and spun the round microphone of the radio they called a prick seven. She'd had to learn so many things quickly. Whittaker depressed the transmit button. "Oscar Papa Two, send it. Over."

"Saber Nine, relay from Glass Palace. Seeker Six established brief uplink. They report significant mechanical issues on the patrol. Recovery requested. They do not have Class Nine and Class Three is critical. Position two decimal five clicks from bottom of Charlie Papa Five. Enemy recon assets may be converging on the area. Quantity and type unknown. Over."

The military discussed everything in an abbreviated fashion, including supply and materiel. Class three referred to fuel and petroleum products. Class nine were repair parts.

"OP Two, how do we know OpFor elements are coming if they can't identify them?"

"Saber Nine, they're reporting biologics scattering behind them. Probably due to fast approach of OpFor, over."

Whittaker's face went from a frown to a scowl. "Good copy, Oscar Papa Two. Relaying to Saber Six. Standby. Saber Nine, out."

Aliza looked him in the eye. "Is everything okay?"

Whittaker shook his head. "I knew being under the command of a guy named Murphy was a bad omen."

"What do you mean?" Aliza asked and then mentally slapped herself. "Oh, I've heard you all talk about Murphy's Law. 'Everything that can go wrong will go wrong.' Yes?"

Whittaker grunted and nudged his mount toward the trail at the top of the rim. "That's about it."

"And things just went wrong?"

He looked over his shoulder. "Things just went to shit, Aliza. There are only two options and neither of them are good."

\* \* \* \*

# Chapter Three

"Halt!" Bo called as soon as he handed the radio handset back to his RTO, Specialist Sublete. He frowned at the wide-eyed young man before turning to the patrol and making eye contact with his leading two section leaders. "Set a coil. Leaders on me."

The riders and their whinnies formed a circular position with their noses pointing out in all directions for security. No one raised a weapon and there was no threat identified, but the simple action kept everyone involved in the patrol's security. All eyes were alert and everyone quiet enough to listen to the surrounding environment. All Bo heard was the blood rushing through his ears in anticipation.

There were two options. The first was the most dangerous—rush the patrol down the trail to the bottom of the pass to rendezvous with Seeker Six's raiding party ASAP to determine how bad things were. But if the enemy came swooping down on them, his small cavalry force wouldn't be able to hold off the attack long enough for reinforcements to arrive.

The second option was the least palatable. Remaining on the high ground gave Bo the freedom of communications with the observation posts and the ability to see and command the field. Staying in place, however, didn't provide security or covering fire to the friendlies limping through the valley toward them. He'd seen far too many soldiers die outside the protection of their nearby units, but the risk to his small force was great. Probably too great.

For a split second, he remembered watching Somalis scampering through alleys with their assault rifles and RPGs to swarm the next convoy from behind. Frantic radio calls to speed up went unheeded or unheard. The leaders of that second convoy had never known why, thirty seconds later and on the block Bo's convoy had just passed through without issue, the vehicles from their nonprofit medical organization were destroyed. With no survivors.

Bo's leaders—the four section leaders, Whittaker, and Turan—gathered. He met Whittaker's questioning eyes. "We move further down, to the next overlook. Set a hasty defensive perimeter. We need to see what the enemy forces are doing. If they're really coming or not."

Whittaker nodded and his facial expression didn't change. "Yes, sir. How are you intending to figure out what the enemy might do?"

"Observation," Bo replied. "And we'll be in radio contact with our guys soon."

"But they're at least a terrain feature away." Sergeant Cook from the first section blurted. "They may be out of sight when an attack comes, sir."

"Noted," Bo frowned. "Look, I'm not happy about this situation either and—"

"We need to go down there," Turan said. "You're leaving them out in the open. Abandoning them."

Jaw clenched, Bo tried to hold back the comment that burst through his lips. "And what would you know about protecting friends in combat, Miss Turan?"

Her eyebrows rose. "What do you mean?"

"How about you leave military operations to those familiar with them? I don't need any advice drawn from your experience as a terrorist," Bo snapped.

Turan stepped forward, her eyes blazing. "You have no idea what I went through, Captain Moorefield!"

"Keep your voice down," Bo replied.

"I will do no such thing. You know nothing about why I did what I did. You cannot imagine what I lost." Her arm shot out and pointed down the hill. "We must go get them!"

Bo wasn't listening. The bluish numbers tattooed on the inside of her arm stunned him silent. He'd not known she was a Holocaust survivor, only that she'd tried to emigrate to Palestine after the war and violently resisted the British authority. His mouth dropped open, and he closed it before looking up at her eyes.

"I had no idea."

"You don't care," she snarled. "Like you don't care for those men out there. You sit here and wait, doing nothing when we should search for water. Medicinals, too. You preach about gathering your—your 'intelligence requirements,' but now, when your men are in great danger, you will not make them the first priority? You will not help them?"

Impatience flashed into anger. Bo stood. The woman took a step back as his hand came up and pointed at her chin. "Make no mistake, Miss Turan, I know there are soldiers down there who need our help, and that supersedes any other mission on this godforsaken planet in this future we didn't want. I'm prepared to do whatever it takes for my friends, and while it might seem contradictory that I am not presently doing so, you are still on this patrol and under my orders. The simple fact is that I *can't* order this patrol to the bottom of the pass until I know more about what we're facing."

She blinked. "But you said that helping them is your priority, that it supersedes—"

"I know!" Bo blurted. "You're missing my point."

Aliza flinched back. "Does this 'point' mean we must sit up here and wait, instead of—?"

"Yes, damn it: that is *exactly* what my point is. I can't risk something catastrophic happening to this untrained and lightly armed unit." It was the truth, but it sounded—and felt—weak; he pushed harder. "Hell, we're little more than a bunch of trainees on mounts with pistols and rifles. If we're going to remain a functional unit, there is no other tactical choice. We set a defense, care for the whinnies, and let the situation develop. Let's make it happen."

The group broke up. Bo turned back toward Scout and prepared to climb into the saddle. The feeling of a stare burning two holes in his back was so strong that he turned around. Aliza Turan's flashing eyes followed his every move. But the voice in his head was not hers.

*You said you cared, and you wanted to make things work, but your actions never showed it. You were too busy waiting for the right time.*

Bo Moorefield sighed and shook off the memory as best he could. He turned and mounted Scout, then moved down the trail with Specialist Sublete to reconnoiter the immediate surroundings. He didn't see Aliza Turan do the same.

\* \* \*

The descent proved more difficult than Aliza first thought. The white and brown scrabble reminded her of the rocky hills of Palestine, although much steeper.

The loose rock made Athena rumble with discomfort as they made their way carefully down the slope and kept a good fifty meters distance from Moorefield and Sublete. Athena shuffled gracefully as the rocks slid out from under her feet before springing to solid rock in a fluid movement that almost took Aliza's breath away.

"Easy, girl," Aliza cooed and patted the lizard-like creature's neck. "Easy."

Reins in hand, she gently guided the whinnie back into the center of the trail while keeping her eyes on Moorefield's back as he made his way down the hill. The whinnie responded like the best dressage horses she'd ridden as a child. The big animal wasted no energy. Every step was fluid and sure. It made every movement with purpose and intent—strong and agile. While a whinnie would never win a dressage competition, there was something about the animal that filled her with joy, and not merely because she had never known so wonderful and exhilarating a riding experience. Mounted on a whinnie's flowing, almost serpentine, back drove away the memories and salved the loss and pain she fought to overcome during every waking moment.

Ahead of her, Moorefield stopped on an outcrop of rock and she instinctively pulled back on Athena's reins.

*Stay here, Aliza.*

The voice was Ben Mazza's, and it threatened to bring tears to her eyes.

His last words to her, before he'd disappeared over the small hillock toward the railway bridge, rung in her heart. The firefight there, between the British and the Palmach, erupted in seconds and caught them by surprise. From their position in over-watch, they had calculated the likelihood of a prepared British response was low. She and Ben carried rifles intending to eliminate any approaching threat as the Palmach moved to plant explosives. The appearance of the British platoon changed the dynamic. Pressed against the dirt with stray bullets whizzing through the air above their heads, she looked into the eyes of the only friend she had in the world.

"Stay here, Aliza." Ben grimaced as machine gun fire tore into the small, narrow valley below. He'd tried to smile at her, but everything in his expression was pained. His dark eyes glittered in the dim moonlight. There was dust in his scruff of beard and dirt on his face. He placed a warm hand on her forearm and nodded once. Before she could respond in kind, or say what she'd wanted to say for weeks, he was gone.

She'd started to follow him when the firefight reached a crescendo. Her memory ended there. She wiped a sleeve at the fresh tear sliding down her left cheek. Eyes squeezed shut, there was nothing she could do for the sudden pain in her chest except to breathe.

A distant, crunching sound from the valley below snapped her attention back to the present. She opened her eyes and nudged Athena forward. Moorefield did not turn around as she approached. His eyes scanned the valley below. As she came alongside, she looked up at him and saw the concerned grimace on his face.

"Miss Turan," he said without looking in her direction.

"What was that noise?" she asked.

Moorefield shook his head. "No idea, but it sounded bad. If the patrol can't get up the pass…" He let the words trail off, and Aliza understood. Anything unable to get up the pass would be left behind, and the raid would have been for naught.

"There has to be something we can do," she challenged, intending to add more. Instead, her eyes caught sight of several small flocks of nameless bird-like animals flapping toward them. As her gaze shifted in that direction, she caught sight of a smudge rising up over the horizon: the unmistakable sign of a dust cloud. "The J'Stull are coming."

"What we do depends on the shape Tapper's guys are in right now," Moorefield said. "Without them, I'm not sure we can do much out here. This patrol would be really outgunned in a direct fight."

"We have to go down there and help them."

Moorefield turned to look at her. He acknowledged her comment with a solemn nod. "I'm sorry for what I said up there."

She looked up into his blue eyes and saw something different. His intense eyes always seemed to stare at something far away, and yet they were softer somehow. More present. "I know you care for those men and women. I shouldn't have said what I said, either."

He looked back at the distant cloud. "I think this day is about to get longer than we ever imagined. So much for finding water and medicinals."

She laughed. "The army conspires against us."

"Captain Moorefield!" Behind them, the RTO approached waving the radio handset. "Sir, update from OP Two. They've got line of sight with the vehicle column now."

She squinted at Moorefield and he saw her expression. "Means our radios can see each other, if that makes any sense."

"It does. I think?" She smiled involuntarily. "What do you want me to do? Take the recruits back to base?"

"Hang on," he replied and reached for the radio handset the moment Specialist Sublete got close enough to hand it over. "Seeker Six, this is Saber Six. SITREP, over."

"Saber Six, we're stopped two klicks from the bottom of the pass. I've got four vehicles non-mission capable at this point."

"Good copy, Seeker Six. Report status of other vehicles."

"Twenty vehicles mission capable. Full loads ammo and fuel. Minimal crews. I have four KIAs and six wounded to get up the pass immediately. Requesting assistance."

Moorefield clenched his jaw for a long moment. As he turned to look at her, the softer look in his eyes was gone and replaced with something she hadn't seen in the young captain before. "Miss Turan, return to Sergeant Whittaker's position. Tell him to have the leaders ready for a mission brief when I get there. I'm going to figure out how to skin this cat."

There was nothing she could say to him. He meant business in every sense of the word. The sudden determination reminded her of Ben and the Palmach soldiers they'd supported. Committed to the task at hand, they would give their all to ensure the others survived. She shelved the uncertainties that persisted in her attitude toward the young officer. He'd trusted her with a task, and she would complete it.

"What are you planning to do?"

Moorefield stared at her, and she realized she liked the confident look on the man. "Whatever it takes."

Aliza snapped the reins. Athena spun in place and trotted forward. They leapt from rock to rock as they climbed up the hill. Once again, Aliza felt the thrill, the joy, of riding the whinnie run through her. It didn't matter that danger was close and everything she knew in this improbable future was at risk. She felt alive again, truly alive.

And she wasn't going to let anything disrupt this second chance at life.

* * *

The rising dust cloud bothered Bo, but not nearly as much as the mechanical breakdown of so many vehicles. Murphy's intent had been to grab everything that they could to assemble combat power. If they could not get the convoy to the top of the pass, amassing the key components of that combat power—specifically, fast vehicles equipped with heavier weapons—would not be an option. While they could attempt to defend their final approach with a mostly infantry force, everything in Bo's experience told him that, whether or not his men had the high ground, it was a bad idea. What they actually needed was that most perishable asset in the universe: time.

*Dammit.*

Bo studied the valley below, noting the higher terrain stretching north and south to his right and left. The flat-topped bluffs resembled the familiar mesas of Colorado and New Mexico. While the vegetation was not the scrub oak and piñon of the higher altitudes, the terrain was not unfamiliar. That's why it had been so easy to choose the ground where they'd established Camp Stark; as on Earth, they sought—and found—a site on the upper reverse slope of a wide tableland with rocky bluffs, cuts, and draws, protecting the summit. There was only one pass wide enough for vehicle travel, and that qualified it as an avenue of approach and key terrain.

*Key terrain.*

Bo wanted to slap himself. He'd been so accustomed to convoy operations in Somalia, following main supply routes back and forth and pulling security against the near targets close by in the rubble and war-torn buildings, that he'd forgotten a simple mnemonic device. OCOKA. Observation. Cover and Concealment. Obstacles. Key Terrain. Avenues of Approach.

*You're an idiot, Bo.* He laughed at himself and studied the terrain around him once more, and a plan formed quickly. He couldn't help but smile.

"You okay, sir?" Sublete asked him.

Bo met the concerned young man's eyes. Sublete, like so many of the others, came from Vietnam and his short career hadn't given him much trust or confidence in officers. "I am, Sublete. Let's get back up the hill. You take the lead."

Once the young soldier had moved a good thirty meters ahead, Bo nudged Scout, and they shot up the trail quickly. Bo looked back over his right shoulder as they passed into the concealment of some vegetation. The dust cloud in the distance had doubled in size.

*No doubt about it. They're coming.*

As they climbed, he adjusted his hands on the reins they'd bought from the indigs with C-rations. He brought his right hand to his mouth and whistled like they had taught him on the farm as a boy. The shrill sound caught the soldier's attention and Bo waved at him to stop in place. As Scout came alongside Sublete's mount, Bo reached out for the radio handset.

"Seeker Six, this is Saber Six. We're coming for you. ETA is fifteen mikes. How copy? Over."

"Saber Six, good copy. We're continuing repair operations and will be ready to move what we can. Seeker Six, out."

\* \* \* \* \*

# Chapter Four

Bo swung out of the saddle into the center of the formation and stepped a few paces away from Scout. With a boot, he cleared a small piece of ground. Kneeling down, he drew the ridgeline they'd descended in the center and then added the path of the mountain pass just to the north of them.

There was a sudden crunch of footsteps rapidly approaching. "Why are you scratching in the dirt?"

Bo looked up and noticed something different. Aliza was talking to him with a little smile on her face. He smiled back. "Miss Turan, we call this a sand table. It's a hasty, visual way to make a plan."

She laughed. "And what are we planning? To save the day?"

*I remember all those times you said you had a plan, but you really didn't. I think you just wanted more time for things to sort themselves out in the hopes the Army would be done with you. You knew they wouldn't, but you kept lying to me about your plans. You and your goddamned plans.*

His own inner voice blotted out the ghost of his ex-wife. *Aliza said "we."*

*We.*

The section leaders gathered. Bo caught the looks on their faces—something between amusement and worry—as they made their way to him. His temper threatened to flare, and he tamped it down. He'd not given them any reason to trust him beyond taking them on mock patrols, so he looked down at the sand table again and took a deep breath.

Whittaker stepped forward. "All accounted for, sir. What's the plan?"

Bo met the older sergeant's eyes and nodded. Without a thought, he fell into the familiar litany of a mission briefing. "We're going after the raiding party. They're stranded at the bottom of the pass with broken-down vehicles and some casualties. I'm taking first and second sections with me. Experienced riders only. For the first phase, we're going down to rendezvous with Seeker Six's lead elements and get a SITREP from them."

Aliza moved to raise her hand, but Whittaker interrupted. "SITREP is a situation report. What's their status and what can we do about it."

Bo kept talking. "Behind us, Sergeant Whittaker and Miss Turan will bring down third and fourth sections. Before you ask, Miss Turan, I can't spare the manpower to take you and the newbies to camp. You're with us and you're in charge of that section. Once we know what the situation is with the Seeker Six's patrol, and their pursuers, we'll plan our next move. We need to see what the bad guys send after our folks, adjust our plan to counter it, and give Camp Stark a chance to evacuate."

"Evacuate?" Turan blurted.

"That's right," Bo replied. "We may have to pull out of Camp Stark and move back toward the area we were reserving for final force consolidation. I'm guessing Major Murphy is already working that piece of the puzzle right now. We'll make sure they prepare the camp to evacuate and beat feet to the rear. That's step six or seven on the list. We've got more important things to handle between now and then."

"You think the…the J'Stull will attack?" Aliza asked.

Bo nodded. "I think they're gonna come after our raiding party with everything they have. But a good cavalry arm always protects the main body. We'll simply do this the old-fashioned way."

Whittaker nodded. "I don't suppose you mean artillery and air support, sir."

"Not at all, Top," Bo replied. "Fire and maneuver. That's really all we have if we can't get those vehicles moving. And we're gonna have to bust our asses to get them to safety."

Whittaker nodded. "Our indig guide never showed, sir."

"A sure sign of an attack," Sergeant Cook remarked under his breath. "I knew we shouldn't have trusted those guys."

Most of the section leaders murmured their assent, though none of them would make eye contact with Bo. They didn't trust anyone but themselves. Bo didn't believe that to be a bad thing, necessarily, but the sergeants didn't seem to trust him or any of the officers, either. He met Whittaker's eyes and the older sergeant nodded confidently at him. He hadn't felt as proud since he'd been a second lieutenant and managed not to screw up being a platoon leader on the first try.

Another crunch sounded in the distance, this time much louder. The whinnies, normally docile and quiet, shuffled and stamped their feet. Two trumpeted nervously. Some newbies appeared on the verge of panic in their saddles, but the more experienced riders all went to their aid and calmed their mounts quickly and, most importantly, quietly.

Aliza spoke up. "The indig: do you think the J'Stull planted him to spy on us? Determine strength and position for the enemy to gauge the attack?"

Impressed, Bo shrugged. "Great question. We don't know. But right now, it doesn't really matter. We have to get down there in order to help the raiding party get those vehicles up onto high ground and back to our compound. If I'm right about the attack, we don't have much time at all." They all nodded, even Turan, which he took as a good sign. Bo pointed at the sand table. "If they hit us while we're moving the vehicles, here's what we're gonna do."

\* \* \*

Bo led the patrol down the mountain as fast as he dared let Scout run. A look over his shoulder proved that both the newbies and the experienced riders were having trouble keeping his pace. Brush tore at his sleeves as Scout bounded down the narrow trail toward the valley floor. Bo relaxed and allowed his hips and lower body to remain attached to the whinnie's side and his body to follow every move the big animal made without expending too much energy. He gave Scout a kick with his right heel, urging him to go faster. The whinnie responded with a lurch forward; Bo snapped backward in the saddle. The nearby flora blurred as Scout accelerated down the steep hill, and Bo smiled and tried not to let out a whoop of excitement.

Barreling through the scrub, they burst onto the valley floor about two hundred meters from the trail leading up the tight pass. Behind a small hill, they were hidden from both the approaching patrol and the enemy. He'd ridden Scout a few times at as full a gallop as the whinnies could go, but bouncing through the brush and from rock outcrop to outcrop left him slightly out of breath, if exhilarated.

Sergeant Cook's section was the first down the trail; his soldiers were all experienced riders. Bo motioned them to move ahead of him and pointed along the base of the hill in the direction of the raiding party. As Cook met his eyes, Bo held up two fingers and pointed them at his eyes. Holding his arm still, he then rotated his fingers to point out, he pointed with his other hand in the direction of the potential enemy patrol. The hand and arm signal to set far side security communicated exactly what Bo wanted them to do without having to either use a radio or use their voices in a tactical environment. Cook and his section of four mounts moved off in the direction he'd indicated.

Second section, under the leadership of Staff Sergeant Stewart, came next. Bo repeated the hand and arm signal, but only pointed at his eyes to indicate near side security. The four mounted soldiers were a mix of experienced riders and newer trainees, but as they galloped toward the convoy, Bo noted that all of their faces were confident and ready.

Third and fourth sections finished their progress down the slope last and almost at the same time, though, technically, he hadn't outfitted a fourth section. Sergeant First Class Whittaker led third section, but with the addition of the newbies under Miss Turan's tutelage, they'd made her a section leader by default, and Whittaker moved those new riders into a fourth section. As they reached level ground, Bo walked Scout out and had them follow behind him. With the security deployed forward, he was again in the lead of the formation as the patrol moved toward the convoy.

Bo heard the convoy before he saw them. The sounds of the vehicles differed vastly from anything he'd heard. Some of them sounded like internal combustion engines. Others sounded like turbines. None of them sounded particularly well-maintained or reliable. As they rounded the ragged bottom of a bluff, Bo stood in his saddle for a first glimpse of them…

And thought, *Well, shit.*

At least three of the vehicles were smoking and one sat askew on the trail, its front end deeply jammed into the loose dirt. Sergeant Stewart appeared to be talking to Lieutenant Tapper. He looked up, saw Bo approaching, and came riding as fast as his whinnie could go.

"Sir!" Stewart reined up the whinnie and skidded to a stop a few meters away. "The El-Tee says they got priority wounded. At least two are critical. They're taking three of the lightest vehicles up the pass to get medical attention. There are seventeen more remaining behind with drivers. Most of them aren't fully crewed."

Bo chewed on the inside of his cheek for a moment. Moving the wounded was the most prudent action they could have taken. "They leaving anyone else behind?"

"Besides the drivers and gunners? A few indig crewmen," Stewart said. "They're trying to get the four dead-lined vehicles moving again."

"Why? What are they?"

"Tacticals." Stewart frowned. The heavy assault vehicles were one of the critical requirements for Tapper's team to capture in their raid. Two bore missile systems and two had multiple rotating machine guns: all weapons that would improve their chances against anyone who might thumb a nose in the Lost Soldiers' direction. Recovering them was a mission requirement.

*Dammit.* "Get back to Tapper and have him get the seventeen ready vehicles into a defensive line, facing those dust clouds. Maximum concealment. Use the terrain and the brush as much as you can. We're gonna figure out a way to get those four busted tacticals up the pass. We'll need everyone else pulling security in case the enemy recon assets fix our position and strike while we're moving those platforms."

Stewart nodded. "How many of the ready vehicles do you want for towing the tacticals, Captain?"

"None."

Stewart flinched as if he'd been struck. "Sir?"

Bo hooked a thumb at the winding, rock-strewn pass behind him. "Look at the width of that pass and the width of those vehicles. Some of them will barely fit. And give their engines a listen, Sergeant. I'm not sure they'll make it up as it is. But towing those tacticals?"

Bo shook his head. "It would be like a go-cart trying to pull a car. One failure and we've got two vehicles blocking the pass. We have to get the tacticals up another way."

Stewart's face clouded. "Begging your pardon, sir, but how?"

"We'll tow them with the whinnies," Bo replied. He had no idea if the whinnies could actually drag the vehicles behind them or not, but the leap seemed logical. Or at least unavoidable. "We may have to tear apart some saddles to get enough rope and cords, but we can do it. Tell Cook to bring in his security as tight as possible and, as soon as the ready vehicles are deployed, find out which of them need crews. On the double."

"You got it, sir," Stewart replied and galloped back toward Cook's position near the bottom of the pass.

Bo looked over his shoulder and caught the eye of his RTO. Sublete moved forward on his mount. "Radio." Sublete passed him the handset. Bo nodded his thanks before holding the ancient piece up to his face like a telephone. "OP One, this is Saber Six. SITREP to relay. Over."

"Copy, Saber Six. Send it."

"Relay to Starkpatch: convoy minus four vehicles secured. Friendlies moving up the pass. Time now. Multiple wounded requiring further evac. Break."

Bo released the transmit button. Whether the J'Stull or anyone else could direction-find their UHF transmissions was an unknown, but prudence said to maintain communications discipline as they always had. And there just wasn't the time to wait for orbital assets to be in a position for secure ground-to-bird and then bird-to-ground relays.

He pressed the switch again, "We are executing recovery operations to move four dead-lined vehicles. Push security elements forward to receive wounded and prepare to support my patrol by indirect fire. I want all mortars on the line and ready to send it. Prepare to execute contingency Charlie. I say again, prepare to execute contingency Charlie. How copy?"

The observation post RTO read back Bo's message verbatim and added, "Saber Six, relay commencing. Please confirm contingency Charlie."

"Contingency Charlie is confirmed. Danger close is authorized, if necessary."

"Copy that, Saber Six. OP Two reports there is biologic activity in your AO and other indications that there is an unknown size force moving this direction from north-northwest. Over."

"Copy," Bo replied. "We've seen it. Report change in size or identification when you can. Saber Six, out."

He handed the handset back to Sublete. "Keep a good ear on that, Sublete. Unless they call for me directly, just relay the information. Stay close. Got it?"

"Will do, sir," Sublete replied. "I'll be your shadow."

Bo grinned. "You do that."

He made a fist, raised it over his head, and brought it down like he was miming it hammering the top of his helmet. The signal for "form on me" brought Whittaker and Aliza Turan forward, their whinnies moving at a trot.

Bo gave them a bare-bones SITREP. When he mentioned the four disabled tacticals, Whittaker raised an eyebrow. Bo nodded grim agreement. "Yep. Gonna be rough. But I think the whinnies could be the answer. Using tow chains, we hitch them two or three per vehicle."

Whittaker's face remained still. "How?"

"We lash together harnesses, using pieces of the newbies' saddles and tack."

"We need those saddles to keep training," Aliza objected.

Bo shook his head. "If these vehicles don't get up the pass and integrated into our overall defenses, we won't have any opportunities to train anyone on anything."

She frowned but did not reply. Her eyes were serious and calm, and she'd taken his comment without a shred of contempt or challenge. Her demeanor suggested that she was prepared to listen to him and act responsibly.

*No, that's not it.* He chided himself as the answer bubbled up: *She's acting like a soldier.* "Can either of you lash? Or weave? Good with knots? Anything to make those harnesses?"

Whittaker grunted. "Willing to bet we have at least one Eagle Scout in the bunch."

"What is that?" Aliza asked and then shook her head. "Not important. We'll make it work."

Bo smiled. "Aliza, some of your newbies may have to dismount and help crew the ready vehicles, anyway. Use their saddles first. See what you can do."

"I will."

Bo looked at Whittaker. "We need two whinnies per tactical, minimum. I want good riders up there, too. If that means we can only send two vehicles at a time, so be it. I want the first ones moving as soon as they're ready."

"What about them?" Whittaker cocked his head toward the rising dust cloud to the north.

Bo looked over his shoulder for a long moment. There really wasn't any option. "First and second sections are providing security now. The minute we get the tacticals moving up the pass, we'll focus on how to skin that cat."

*Or maybe, kill it.*

\* \* \*

Whittaker had been correct. Two of the newbies, a private from the American contingent of Vietnam vets and one of the Brits had been Scouts and knew their way around ropes and straps. Aliza watched them strip saddle materials and reins, tie them into ropes, and rig up makeshift harnesses for two of the largest whinnies. She watched as Moorefield and Whittaker set about hooking them up to the lead tactical. The first whinnie, with a black-tipped tail, stepped into the trail and backed into the harness with ease. A darker male with a crimson blaze on its angular forehead took some coaxing, but finally, anxiously, backed into position. With quick work and quiet, purposeful direction from Moorefield, they tied the harnesses into place. The young captain clearly had experience working with animals, and the whinnies were surprisingly compliant.

The riders nudged the whinnies and the tow straps snapped tight as they strained against the weight of the broken-down vehicle. Its wheels inched forward. A cheer erupted from the group as the whinnies pulled harder, gaining momentum.

"Hey! Step in there and push it," Moorefield ordered a group of soldiers standing nearby. "Get them moving faster."

The soldiers stepped behind the vehicle and put their hands and shoulders into it. The vehicle rolled forward faster and faster. The black-tailed whinnie snorted a call and leaned into the weight hard, its head low to the ground. Almost immediately, the darker male did the same and the rate of the vehicle's forward progress doubled and then doubled again. They were moving up the steepening hill at a good pace.

"Stay behind it!" Bo pointed at the soldiers pushing the vehicle. "All the way to the top."

Whittaker's voice boomed nearby. "Get the second vehicle hooked up!"

Aliza watched the first vehicle move up the pass and then almost disappear when it went around the first curving switchback. While the towing appeared to work well, it was slow. Too slow. She nudged Athena and walked over to Moorefield. His eyes followed the effort to hook up the second vehicle and get it moving.

"This is too slow," she said in a low voice. "We won't get all of them up the pass."

He turned to her with a frown on his face. "I know. We just have to do the best we can, Aliza."

She didn't respond. His casual use of her first name sent a ripple of excitement down her spine. Her own reaction shocked her—until she started at a whinnie bellowing directly behind her.

Aliza spun to see one of the more experienced riders holding on to his saddle for dear life as his whinnie bucked and thrashed in the makeshift harness. Several soldiers shouted commands and advice, but there was panic all over the rider's face and he half-fell and half-jumped clear. He hit the dirt, rolled, and scrambled away from the whinnie. Without its rider, the animal calmed down, but twisted and shook like a wet dog, trying to throw off the ropes connecting it to the second disabled vehicle.

Moorefield dismounted his whinnie and ran toward the distressed one. A few meters away, he stopped, and she could hear his low voice talking calmly. She lost his words in the slight breeze and the ambient noise around her. His whinnie, still at her side, trumpeted softly and a few others repeated the noise with their own distinct voices. The anxious whinnie calmed, stamped two of its feet in rapid succession, and then turned to stare unpleasantly at Moorefield as he stepped closer.

* * * * *

# Chapter Five

When he was eighteen, Bo and his father took in three horses from a neighboring farm that had fallen into disrepair. The lush green fields of northern Mississippi gave the animals enough in their pasture to eat, but they hadn't had real interaction with human beings in the several months of their previous owner's illness. When Bo and his dad arrived, the old mare of the group trotted over happily and let them get a lead onto her without much trouble. The other two horses stayed a good hundred meters away, eyeing them warily.

It took more than an hour to get the older male calmed down and led to the gate. The younger stud stomped in circles as Bo talked to it like his father always did. His father leaned against the front fender of the old Ford truck and watched for an hour as Bo tried and failed repeatedly. Disgusted, he'd walked over, leaned a hip against the nearest headlight, and spat. His father smiled.

As Bo stared down the whinnie, he heard his father's voice as clear as ever. *No two animals are the same, Bo. What works for one doesn't always work for the other.*

With Scout, he'd never raised his voice or violently spurred the animal. The whinnie had always responded. The anxious one appeared to take little notice of Bo's attempt at soothing words. He stayed quiet and walked forward confidently and slowly. The whinnie watched him approach and stilled.

*Easy.* He didn't say the word aloud; it was more a matter of *willing* it at the big lizard. *Easy, boy.*

The whinnie looked up and over Bo's head. He resisted the urge to follow the animal's gaze; he stepped forward and grabbed the reins. When the whinnie didn't respond, Bo grabbed the saddle and swung himself up into the seat in one smooth motion. That was when he saw that the whinnie's eyes were on Scout, twenty meters away. Who stood alert and staring at the whinnie he'd climbed aboard. The intensity of Scout's eyes struck him.

*They're not just smart. They're almost—or actually?—intelligent.*

In the next breath, he mentally shook himself. Intelligent wasn't necessarily the word he was looking for: they were sentient. They communicated verbally with their hoots and other noises. Like horses, they moved as a herd. Maybe they even had alphas and omegas. Societal instincts, intelligence, and communication spoke to something much more than they'd assumed the whinaalani to be. His mind reeling at the discovery, Bo forced himself back to the present and backed the whinnie into position for the harness.

He pointed at Stewart. "Hook him up."

The sergeant and two others did so quickly. "Good to go, sir."

Bo leaned back in the saddle and looked over at the other rider, Specialist Davis. "You ready?"

Davis, a tall and lanky Alabaman, nodded and drawled. "On you, sir."

Before he could respond, Specialist Sublete waved at him. "Sir, the first vehicle has reached the top of the pass."

Bo replied, "Tell them I'm on my way with the second. I'll get back here as fast I as can. Sergeant Whittaker, you're in charge until I get back. Let's see just how much time we have."

Before he nudged the whinnie into action, he caught sight of the dust cloud along the northern horizon. It had doubled in size against R'Bak's sky.

*Let's hope it's enough.*

\* \* \*

As Moorefield and Davis disappeared around the first bend of the trail with six soldiers pacing them on foot, Aliza caught Sergeant Whittaker's eye. The old soldier sat astride his mount, Casper, staring at the dust cloud.

"Are you okay?" she asked.

He nodded once and looked back beyond her to the horizon. "The better of the four vehicles are headed up the pass. That means we're fifty percent complete with this part of the mission."

"That's a good thing, isn't it?"

He laughed. "In ordinary circumstances, yes. This isn't ordinary. Looks like we've got the whole damned J'Stull army headed this direction. And we're forward, located away from the rest of our own ground forces. Gonna be a long day."

She followed his eyes to the dust cloud. There was no doubt the J'Stull were coming now. Word was that Tapper and his team had hit the enemy hard. The enemy would not merely want to eliminate their attackers, but make examples of them and, so, would accelerate across the valley floor. She looked over the defensive line of vehicles—all random shapes and weapons—and wondered how they could hold off an assaulting force of any size.

"Is he thinking about using those vehicles down here instead of moving them up the pass? I don't think they have a prayer of delaying the J'Stull, no matter how well we fight them."

"When the time comes, we'll do what we have to do, Aliza." Whittaker sighed. He spun his mount and called to Sergeant Stewart. "Set one hundred percent security. Push out a section to recon the north side of the pass, but no farther than Phase Line Sheridan."

Aliza squinted at him. "What is a phase line?"

He laughed. "A control measure. We call it a phase line, which, in this case, is an intermittent creek bed about two klicks north. Giving it a code helps us relay information faster."

"And Sheridan?"

"American Civil War general, Union side." Whittaker grinned. "He was the quintessential cavalryman. Very colorful guy."

"Why use his name?"

Whittaker's grin faded. "He's one of Captain Moorefield's favorite generals. Gave the Confederates fits in West Virginia. Unpredictable and elusive. Exactly the guy we could use right now."

"And is Moorefield 'that guy?'" she asked.

Whittaker shrugged. "Could be. But he's gotta have the heart for it."

Aliza wondered what the sergeant meant but did not have time to ask as Whittaker rode out to set the patrol into their duties.

\* \* \*

The ride to the top of the pass went more smoothly than Bo would have dared to imagine. Once the whinnies snapped the towlines taut, they kept a constant, measured pace all the way up the two-kilometer trail. As they crested the top, Bo sent the walkers down the pass. Bo intended to join them as quickly as the recovery team from the camp could unhook the vehicle.

Fortunately, Lieutenant Meehan had come through. The recovery team—a half-dozen mechanics and maintenance specialists with two vehicles from the motor pool—came forward with heavier tow chains. A squad of infantry was detailed to both sides of the trail, standing security. As soon as Bo and Davis had the crippled tactical over the lip and on mostly flat ground, the recovery team unhooked the hasty harnesses, draped them over the front of the two riders' saddles, and started connecting the chains. The two strange vehicles—crude diesel command car-truck hybrids—rumbled to life, belching black exhaust into the air as they backed toward the tactical to put a little extra slack in the chains. Once attached, the recovery team mounted up, and the first vehicle gunned its engine, building the torque required to tow it swiftly to the rear. The smell of diesel exhaust never failed to bring back memories of the first time Bo had climbed aboard an Abrams main battle tank at Fort Knox. What he would have given for a few of those beautiful beasts on R'Bak. The ability to see, positively identify, and then engage targets thousands of meters away would have been a beautiful thing.

As the first recovery vehicle started towing the tactical away, Bo turned to Davis. "Get down the hill with these harnesses. Get the next one ready." The young specialist pivoted his mount and galloped back toward the men readying the last two vehicles. Bo glanced around, found the RTO for the security patrol Meehan had sent, and waved him over, making a "give me" motion as he reached for the handset. "Starkpatch, this is Saber Six. Fifty percent of the disabled tacticals are on the plateau. We're heading back for the rest now. Over."

"Saber Six, be advised. OP Two says enemy forces are heading that way. Not sure you'll have time to recover them all. Over," Meehan replied.

"They are mission imperative. We're not leaving them." Bo frowned. "We'll just have to move faster, Starkpatch."

"Sir, all due respect, you can't buy time you don't have."

"The hell I can't," Bo snarled into the handset. "Saber Six, out."

With a nod at the RTO, Bo whirled the whinnie back toward the trail. This male didn't respond like Scout did, but it moved well enough, and fast enough, to settle Bo's mind to the task at hand.

*You can't buy time you don't have.*

A force of unknown strength was bearing down on them. His cavalry patrol couldn't fight them off, and the retreat from Camp Stark back to the main assembly area was poised to start. If the enemy kept coming at the rate Bo thought they were, even the retreat could fail. The paltry forces forward at Camp Stark, or any of the other smaller posts Murphy had set out for different missions, wouldn't be able to develop a concerted defense. Everything dirt-side was in danger.

*I have to buy time.*

As quickly as the thought crossed his mind, he smiled. It could be done. All he had to do was sell it to Sergeant Whittaker and Aliza Turan. She'd wanted to check out the higher ground for trails and viable passes. Well, now she would have her chance.

When he turned the corner at the bottom of the pass, Bo saw the dust cloud from the enemy advance rising higher than before. He caught sight of his patrol hooking up the third vehicle under the watchful eyes of Aliza and Whittaker. As he closed the gap, he saw her looking at him and his stomach churned. She would not like what he had in mind. Using her and the bulk of the patrol—the rest of the newbies—as bait didn't set well with him. Something in his gut said she would like it even less, and he realized that was exactly why it bothered him.

\* \* \*

"You want me to *what?*" Aliza asked Moorefield, dumbfounded. She raised her palms to him. "Just so I understand you, please."

The young captain licked his lips and started again. "You and Sergeant Whittaker will take your sections north along the skirts of the tableland at a gallop. I want you to raise as much dust as you can and make the enemy think there's more of us with you than over here at the pass. A *lot* more. It will buy us additional time to get these last two vehicles up to the recovery team."

She shook her head and a nervous laugh came out. "You're making a big assumption."

"More than one; I am aware," he replied. "But the whinnies *will* find a way up into the middle slopes at the edge of the plateau. All you have to do is to attract the enemy's attention for fifteen minutes. The whinnies will do the rest. When the J'Stull turn and chase you, we'll counterattack into their exposed flank."

"And what about when the enemy storms our position on the slopes of the tableland, Captain Moorefield? What then?" The anger in her voice surprised her, but she'd seen firsthand the consequences of poor planning and uneven execution.

"You let me handle that, Aliza." He lowered his chin and frowned, but there was still a twinkle in his eye. "Whittaker has command. All you and the newbies have to do is make your patrol look like a herd of elephants."

"And if we don't find a way up?"

"You will. We'll be there before they can attack you with any strength, I promise."

The calm, confident look on his face and the slow smile threatening to crease it made Aliza smile involuntarily. A sudden grit-laden gust made her blink and sweep her hair away from her face in one movement. When she opened her eyes, not more than a second had passed, and he was still looking at her in the same manner. In the next heartbeat, she realized that she liked it, and it only made her smile wider.

"Well…" She paused. "We'll have to raise some dust and find a way up between the cliffs."

His smile widened and his teeth shone. "You do that, Aliza. We're counting on you."

She nodded. "We won't let you down."

"Trust the whinnies," he blurted. She frowned, not certain what he meant. "I think they're smarter than we realize."

She squinted at him. "In what way?"

"When I took that other mount…well, whatever Scout and Athena vocalized got through to it. I'm pretty sure I wasn't the one who calmed him."

"They *are* very vocal animals," she replied, but the rest of the thought stopped on her lips. They'd casually assumed control over the whinaalani, as if they were little more than clever farm animals trained to submit to human dominance. She took in a breath in a sudden flash of realization. "What if we've gotten them all wrong?"

Moorefield nodded and took a long breath. His voice was low when he said, "I think we have from the very start. I'm not sure if they understand what we're saying to them, but I think they understand our emotions somehow."

"That's fascinating." She shook her head even as recollections of Athena's behaviors when being ridden and called played through her memory, like quick clips from a newsreel; the speed and surety of her responses were unlike any horse she'd even known. "You think they are sentient?"

He shrugged. "I don't know. Honestly, we don't have time to think about it. Just trust them. Get ready to move out as soon as Sergeant Whittaker is ready."

"Yes, Captain."

"Thank you." He tipped the brim of his boonie hat and nodded to her. "Just one more thing? Call me Bo."

He turned away to direct his soldiers. Heart trip-hammering in her chest, Aliza turned back to Athena and heard the distinct purring sound the female whinaalani made when content. Athena's angular head turned toward her; the wide, dark eyes studied her for a moment before their focus turned back to the others. Soldiers from the third and fourth sections who'd dismounted to assist with the tow operation climbed aboard their whinnies. Across the road, Whittaker spoke with Moorefield and pointed first in the direction of the game trail they'd used to descend from the tableland and then out across the ragged bluffs to the north and east.

"Third and fourth sections, mount up," she heard Whittaker call. She climbed aboard Athena smoothly and nudged the whinnie toward the soldiers. Astride Scout once again, Moorefield trotted toward her.

"One more thing," he called.

"Yes?"

His lips were a tight, thin line. "If Sergeant Whittaker asks you to do something, please do it. There will be a good reason he's asking. I know you've had some experience in the field, but this is one time I can't have you not following Top's orders—or even his advice or requests. So if, for example, he tells you to stay somewhere, we need you to stay the hell there. Do you understand, Aliza?"

A bolt of electricity shot down her spine. Aliza's mouth fell open, and she snapped it closed. With a nod, she acknowledged Moorefield's request without trusting herself to speak. Her words wouldn't have been something she could explain in the time they had. Try as she might, she could not stop hearing Ben Mazza's voice insisting she do the same thing, just before he'd disappeared over the hill above the Nahal Kziv.

And never came back.

* * *

Bo watched the screening party under Whittaker and Aliza gallop east along the edge of the bluffs. He hoped they would quickly find a viable route up the steep sides of the tableland. He chuckled. "Hope" was not a term he associated with combat. His last Army squadron commander, before he'd done his tour in Mogadishu, had been a career light infantryman placed in charge of a cavalry unit almost against his will. His view of mounted operations skewed far into the negative range. Lieutenant Colonel Peabody wasn't a negative person, but his view of things was both realistic and memorable. Among his favorite sayings was that hope was not a method. No real come-back for that axiom, Bo admitted.

He gave the departing patrol one last long glance and then turned back to the towing operation, intent on getting the last two vehicles up the hill as quickly as the first two so he could support—and protect—his screen as soon as possible.

Sublete was waiting, radio handset outstretched as Bo turned in his direction. "Sir? OP Two."

Bo took the handset from Sublete. "Saber Six, go."

"Saber Six, OP Two. Relay from orbital assets via Glass Palace. Regimental-sized enemy force moving your direction. Estimated distance to your location is twenty-three kilometers. Estimated speed of lead elements is forty-one kilometers per hour. ETA to you is less than three zero minutes. Acknowledge. Over."

The gnawing sensation in his gut threatened to burgeon into nausea.

"OP Two, roger. Relay to Glass Palace: acknowledged. We are Charlie Mike. Over." Charlie Mike meant continuing the mission. He'd picked up the slang from the Vietnam veterans and, while not established procedure, it seemed to fit best.

"Saber Six. Acknowledged and wilco. Out."

*Thirty minutes.*

*Shit.*

There wasn't time to lament the timing or the situation. The third stalled vehicle, towed by two whinnies and their riders from the second section, strained against the straps for a moment before the broken platform rolled forward slowly.

Bo watched the creeping progress. Every rotation of the platform's wheels produced a squealing sound.

"Sounds like a bad bearing. Maybe a few," Sublete said.

"You have a maintenance background?"

The young sandy-haired soldier shook his head. "Not in the army, sir. But around the farm, everything had a bad bearing at one time or another."

Bo nodded and analyzed the entire operation for a moment and tried not to wince. The pace of the third vehicle was nothing like the previous two. Bo calculated the two whinnies had towed both previous vehicles up the pass in less than fifteen minutes. That would not be the case with the remaining two tacticals.

"Sergeant Cook?" Bo called over to the section leader. "Get the last one tied up and moving. We're short on time. Might be tight up there, but it's necessary to reduce the interval."

"Aw, hell," Bo heard Sublete mutter under his breath.

He glanced toward the moving vehicle and saw that its forward momentum was half of what it had been in the loose soil. Even with four soldiers pushing it at ground level, the vehicle barely moved forward.

"Cook! Get a third whinnie on that vehicle. Push it if you have to."

"Copy, sir." The young sergeant whirled his mount and called for another whinnie and rider to get behind the vehicle and push. As awkward as that position was, the whinnie used its chest and left front leg to grab the rear of the platform near the ammunition supply deck and pushed. Moving on three legs didn't seem to bother the animal, and several of the other whinnies made low, rumbling sounds. Bo heard and felt Scout make the same sound, and he instinctively patted the animal's neck.

"You like what you're seeing, don't you?" Bo said in a low voice. "You get us, don't you? I don't think you know what we're saying, but you get it, huh?"

Scout turned his long neck hard to the left and faced Bo for a short moment. He snorted once and returned his gaze to the towing of the third platform, as did Bo. It was moving at a better pace, made the first switchback turn, and headed up the winding, two-kilometer trail. Bo looked around. There were a few indigs and soldiers left from the raiding party along with two whinnies from the second section and himself. It would have to be enough.

"C'mon, Scout." Bo nudged his mount toward the rear of the fourth vehicle. "We're gonna do the same thing, buddy. Give it a push."

Scout moved forward without being nudged, and Bo shook his head. Murphy and the others needed to know what they'd discovered. There was no doubt the whinnies understood the situation. Several of them stamped their feet anxiously.

*If we had more harnesses, we could lash up a whole damned team of them. That would get these things moving.*

"Hey, sir?" Sublete called behind him. "That one's in pretty bad shape."

Bo glanced back over his shoulder. "The vehicle? What's wrong with it?"

"Sir, I ain't sure it's gonna move much at all," Sublete said. "Both of the back wheels look shot and the axle is bent. Looks like it took a hit or two on the retreat. Got shot up good."

Bo turned back to the vehicle and saw exactly what Sublete meant. He hadn't had the time to give the vehicles more than a cursory look at first. But as luck—*or Murphy's Law?*—would have it, the first two vehicles had been the good ones. It was the last two that were much worse for wear. In fact, where the rear axle should have run straight through the rear of the fourth vehicle's frame, there was a definite curve.

*The damned thing's gonna wobble like one of those wooden duck toys.* Bo shook his head. *We're lucky it made it this far.*

"Sergeant Cook!" Bo yelled. "Give me one rider back here. We're gonna double the push on this one with the whinnies."

"Yes, sir," Cook replied and spun his own whinnie toward the soldiers who remained at the base of the trail.

Bo looked over the dismounted troops left from the raiding party: they looked tired and dehydrated, but still ready. "You men, get moving. Stay between these two vehicles in case we need your help to recover them. Lock and load. Grab anything else that needs to get up the trail and move out."

Scout took his position next to another whinnie, a lighter-colored female, behind the fourth vehicle. With two whinnies in front and two behind, the vehicle lurched forward and moved up the trail. It wobbled worse than Bo had predicted, but it kept moving. After a minute, they lurched into the first of the winding turns, clearing the close rock outcroppings on either side by scant inches. Bo risked a glance at his ancient ticking watch.

*We're gonna make it.*

* * * * *

# Chapter Six

Away from the tight draw where the main trail ascended to the lip of the tableland, the scrub brush thinned. At the head of the column, Aliza saw Whittaker gesture with his arms out like wings and the rest of the experienced riders swung outward in a triangular formation the soldiers called a wedge. As she rode, she saw at least a couple of her section looking at her for instruction or direction. She repeated the same gesture as Whittaker at the front of the formation. Her section of six riders swept out behind her in a similar wedge of their own, doubling the amount of dust kicked up by the formation.

She couldn't help but grin. Athena galloped forward at a steady, manageable pace, and the sensation she was truly and absolutely free washed over her. R'Bak was a far cry from southern Germany, but that didn't matter. In fact, maybe that helped. For the first time since Palestine, she felt like she belonged. The joy of their ride was palpable. Every time she'd been astride a whinnie, she'd almost forgotten about Dachau.

Back on Earth, all she'd wanted to do was go home, but there hadn't been a home. She'd listened to Ben Mazza and others that their future was in Palestine, but ultimately that hadn't even been an option. Alive in a future so removed from that earlier time and place, it was easier to simply focus on moving as one with Athena and, for the first time in as long as she could remember, being in and enjoying the moment. Just that and nothing else.

The dust cloud to the west continued to grow. Riding hard, they kept a steady pace that would have fatigued a modern horse within twenty minutes. They pushed north, following the near vertical face of the tableland's margin. Red-orange cliffs glowed in the light of R'Bak's star. Along the edges, at almost symmetrical distances, bluffs extended from the escarpment into the lower plains. Whether wind, water, or something else had carved them, the rocky spurs shielded at least a part of the terrain between each. One of those tight, dark draws had to have a trail up to the tableland and from there, a way home.

*A way home.*

That she considered R'Bak and the Lost Soldiers as her home didn't strike Aliza as ironic. It was a progression, of sorts. Acceptance of the fate dealt to her was no small task. Yet, with no one around her dedicated to the project of exterminating her and the people from which she was descended, there was hope, once again. And as long as there was hope, she remembered her father saying often, there was light. And light would always prevail.

*Given time and heart, Aliza, anything is possible.*

Racing east along the bluffs, Aliza saw Whittaker turn his whinnie to the right, toward one of the rocky bluffs. There was enough of a curvature to the hump of rock that a pass, whether washed out by erosion or something else, was likely. That would give them a way up to the higher ground. Above the draw, the pitch of the terrain increased to near vertical in places. If they could get up there, the enemy might not give chase. In the shadows of the morning light, there seemed to be some open areas near the bluff. Perhaps they were even enough to maneuver around and through.

Aliza felt her mount pivot toward the draw without any pressure on the reins and grinned. Bo was right. They knew. Somehow, the big friendly animals knew more about humans and their intentions than should have been possible.

*Let's hope that's enough to save the day.*

\* \* \*

A kilometer up the pass, the tight scrub brush along either side of the trail dwindled enough that Bo could see the entire northern horizon. What he saw chilled him. The dust cloud marking the enemy's approach hadn't only doubled in size, but it appeared to be broad enough that it might still span the distance between the ready vehicles and his patrol, and the screen line being raised by Whittaker and Turan's rapid transit across the front of the tableland. Time was always the most perishable resource in a combat operation, and now, with the enemy already maneuvering to intercept, it was against them.

"Sublete!" he called over his shoulder. The RTO had taken up a position a few meters behind the center of the vehicle that Bo and Scout were pushing from the left rear. "Call OP One. They are to fall back up the game trail and plot TRPs along the way. Authorize them to call for fire as necessary. I want our mortars covering that pathway. Got it?"

"Word for word, sir," Sublete replied. Almost immediately, Bo heard the young radio operator giving OP One the instructions to shutter their operations forward and race back to the tableland proper. Target reference points would provide the limited mortar support from the rear with a means of rapidly zeroing in on that likely avenue of approach. Every single way up the tableland's escarpment had been targeted, just like the pass they had been operating in. Every good defensive plan provided a contingency to deal with every possible avenue of attack. In this case, they had to rely upon mortars.

The only other way to deter enemy advances would have been mine-fields and obstacle emplacements, but they hadn't had the time, sup-plies, or equipment for those. The lack of emplaced obstacles was particularly unfortunate because that meant there was no way to slow down attackers. The only option was to distract and lure them into a pre-selected engagement area. Assuming Whittaker and Turan found a way back up to the top of the tableland. And assuming it was a place where contingency Charlie could be applied to maximum ef-fect.

Scout shuffled in the loose soil and rock of the path, and the ve-hicle's forward progress hitched. The other whinnies at their side and the two in front strained and kept the vehicle moving. Bo felt rather than saw Scout get his feet under him. The big whinnie leaned against the broken vehicle with an audible grunt that sounded dis-tinctly angry. Bo couldn't help but smile.

"C'mon, Scout." He leaned down over the whinnie's neck. "You got this, buddy."

The second switchback up the trail—at roughly the halfway point of the two-kilometer journey—was the narrowest part. The two tow-ing whinnies rode shoulder-to-shoulder as they made the turn. Bo and Sergeant Cook struggled to fit their mounts in the space. Large rock formations shielded both sides of the trail, pinching its width down to three meters. To make matters worse, the pitch of the trail increased to a good seven percent incline. Back on Earth, powerful tractor-trailers with full loads struggled to make it up that kind of hill. The wobbling axle ground against both wheels and the vehicle lurched in multiple directions at once.

"Yah!" To his right, Bo saw Cook kick his whinnie hard in the side. Nothing changed. His mount was working as hard as it could to shove the vehicle with its left foreleg while digging its rear legs into the dirt for any kind of purchase. "Yah!"

The mount trumpeted again, and Bo heard Scout snort loudly and flinch his neck to look over his shoulder. The flash of anger caught Bo off guard, but he understood. They were doing all they could and didn't need outside encouragement.

"Cook!" Bo leaned over. "Don't kick her again."

Cook's entire face was a question. "Sir?"

"They're giving it all they can already. They're not like horses or mules." Bo pointed at his reins. "When's the last time you really had to guide her?"

"What do you mean, sir?"

"Have you done a damned thing to get her to put a shoulder into that vehicle? To push with three legs like that? Did you even think that was possible?"

Cook's face regained composure and realization at the same instant. "Oh, shit! Er...Sir. You're right."

Scout trumpeted softly. Bo wondered if he meant to say something like "Finally." Or maybe Scout had recognized that the entire unit at Camp Stark seemed to use "Oh, Shit" as their motto.

"Let them do their thing. All we gotta do is—"

Metal squealed as the axle bent sharply near the left rear wheel. The gun platform crashed into the dirt just as Bo and Scout, driving forward and right behind the wheel, saw it shear away. The sound was similar to an explosion, so loud that the whinnies flinched. Scout, leaning heavily into the vehicle, only had enough time to flinch backward.

Bo couldn't seize the reins fast enough. There was the brief sensation of flying backward, untethered through the air until he hit the ground. And then—

Nothing.

* * *

*D*o you remember that night at the enology lab? Out in the vineyard? I do. I remember the clouds were indigo in the reflected city lights. The rains were long gone, and we sat out there on a blanket and watched soundless lightning race along the underside of the thunderheads up toward Tupelo. You tried so hard to be romantic. Roses and wine. It was sweet, but for a second date it wasn't much. You asked me about it later. Why hadn't I been ready to kiss you? Do you remember where we went after that? That I needed to drop off an assignment at Justin's apartment? And he wasn't there, so we went back to my apartment and watched a movie?

*I think about that night a lot. If Justin had been there, I wouldn't have come back to your car. I wouldn't have gone out with you anymore. I shouldn't have kept going because I knew. I thought—I told myself—you were good enough.*

*But I knew better.*

\* \* \*

*B*o came awake with a start, wiping at his warm, wet face frantically and checking his palm for blood. Instead, he saw thick globs of clear liquids filled with the tiny bubbles of spittle. Above him, Scout was staring down at him with an expectant, if not concerned, look on his angular face. The whinnie made a deep-throated sound oddly like a cat's purr and stepped back as Bo sat up, rubbing the back of his head.

"Easy, sir." Sergeant Cook was at his side with a compress. "You've got a nasty knot back there, but no blood. You okay?"

As he sat up, the world swam from left to right and back again violently. He blinked several times in succession to clear his vision. The pain began as a small buzz and grew until it filled his head and threatened to block out everything.

"How long was I out?"

Cook shrugged. "Less than a minute. Gave us a good scare, though. Never seen a whinnie get so scared, either. He was all over you, licking your face and scratching the ground. I think you're right about them, sir. I think they really care for us."

Bo nodded and instantly regretted the slight movement of his head. He blinked again, and his dizziness abated. "Help me up," he asked Cook. The sergeant stood and extended a hand, which Bo took. As he stood, Bo felt better but still wobbly. He'd hit his head plenty on armored vehicles and knew the feeling and how to operate with it. He rubbed the back of his head and gingerly probed the swollen spot. It wasn't an open wound, but he'd still need it checked.

"Bird went with the first vehicle, didn't he?" Bo asked. The diminutive medic was nowhere in sight.

"Yes, sir."

Bo laughed. "Dammit. You don't have any aspirin, do you?"

Cook shook his head. "You want me to send for Bird? He can get back down here and throw it over to us from the other side of the wreck."

"No time," Bo grunted.

He studied the collapsed tactical that was wedged solidly in the middle of the tight trail. There was no way it would move in any direction without divine intervention or serious explosives.

"Mission failure," he said and spat in the R'Baku dirt.

"That ain't your fault, sir." Cook replied.

"The hell it's not." Bo fought the urge to kick at the dirt he'd spat in.

"We did the best we could," Cook offered.

Bo slapped at the dirt on his legs with both hands. "We should have gotten down the pass faster."

Cook said nothing in response. He didn't have to. The commander was always the one to blame. No matter if his intentions were honorable and good. The mission had been to recover the entire raiding party and the vehicles they'd secured. Of paramount interest were the gun platforms, and while twenty-three out of twenty-four wasn't bad, they were not going to get the final vehicle up the pass. For Bo, that was tantamount to failure.

"Saber Six, this is OP Two, over."

Bo gestured for Sublete and the radio handset, reached up for it with a grunt, and got a fresh bolt of dull, throbbing pain down his spine. "Saber Six, go."

"Saber Six, we've got visual contact with lead enemy elements. Estimate they're fifteen klicks out and have slowed their advance. The lead formation has sighted the screen and diverted almost fully in that direction. How copy?"

Bo took a breath and held it for a moment before releasing it. The plan was working so far. "Good copy, OP Two. What else?"

"Sir, confirming the lead element is a regimental-sized force. Two battalions are line abreast in the front of the formation."

Bo blinked. "Say again your last?"

The RTO repeated the report and Bo almost wobbled back to the ground. A *regiment*? Heading straight toward Sections Three and Four? He exhaled slowly. He'd been right; this was not a cat he'd be able to skin. This was a cat he had to kill. He nodded, depressed the key on the handset. "Copy, OP Two. Relay that SITREP to Stark-patch, coded for immediate relay to Glass Palace. Relay to Saber Nine, I am en route with reinforcements. Time now. Saber Six, out."

He ran his fingers through his sweaty hair and realized his hat was missing. In the intense radiation of R'Bak's two stars, skin cancers and melanoma were all too real a possibility. He turned a slow circle and found his boonie hat. With the care and patience of a much older man, he bent forward and grabbed it from the ground. As he stood up to his full height, the pain and the wobbling sensation weren't anywhere near what they had been before. His adrenaline had kicked in at the most opportune time. If they didn't get a move on, his idea to counterattack the J'Stull as they chased the screen wouldn't materialize.

Bo took a quick breath and exhaled it just as quickly to clear his mind and felt one of his ears pop involuntarily. He shook his head, albeit gently, and looked up at Cook who was the only senior leader on the downhill side of the vehicle.

"Get everyone on the other side of the wreck up the pass, right now. Send a mount to the vehicles. Tell them to stand by and not start any engines until I tell them to. We're gonna ride for the screen and hope like hell they've found a pass."

Cook nodded and bounced his whinnie up to the vehicle and called over the platform for the others to fall back to the vehicles. As he looked around, Bo counted: Cook, Sublete and their whinnies were with him on the downslope from the wreck. Four soldiers from the raiding party and two indig guides were with them as well. He gestured at them and then back down the trail. "Double up on the whinnies and get to the bottom ASAP. Mount up on a vehicle and get ready to attack. We're not playing defense anymore."

Seeing the dismounted troops scramble aboard the available mounts took some of the weight of command off his shoulders. He raised the handset again. "OP Two, the pass is blocked. Personnel upslope of the block are recovering in your direction. Report when they rendezvous with recovery forces. Break."

He released the transmit button and then pressed it again two seconds later. Old habits died hard. "Relay to Saber Nine, we're en route. Need their location and route. Over."

"Saber Six, OP Two. Good copy. Will relay to Saber Nine when we can see them again. Over."

"You don't have eyes on them now?" Bo asked, incredulous.

"Negative, sir. We haven't seen them for over ten minutes. They're too close to the bluffs down there. Lost radio contact at the same time. Over."

Bo ran a hand over his face and placed his tongue between his teeth as though intending to bite his words back. He had failed.

"Sonuvabitch!"

* * * * *

# Chapter Seven

As Athena bolted up the narrow gap and bounced from outcrop to outcrop, Aliza clenched the reins with every ounce of strength in her hands. She clamped her legs in the saddle to hold her in position atop the whinnie. Hands and legs burned from the effort, she realized she'd been holding her breath. Forcing herself to breathe, Aliza bounced in the makeshift saddle again as Athena scrambled toward, and then up, a vertical face only a few meters high. Aliza gasped at the speed and audacity of the move. The speed of the climb shocked her. On the mostly flat, rocky ground of the tableland and surrounding desert, the animals were graceful and fast. But she'd seen no evidence of the almost gravity-defying climbing ability that Athena was demonstrating. Slipping over the top of the wall in less than three seconds, the whinnie moved uphill and deeper into the brush, the other whinnies trailing behind her.

Aliza pulled back gently on the reins. "Slow down, girl. Let's wait for the others."

Athena grunted and continued moving forward at a slow walk. The whinnie didn't want to slow down but understood Aliza's intent. As they climbed up the hill through the scrub brush, the narrow passage around the craggy bluff opened onto a wider area. While the brush seemed thicker and more pervasive, Aliza realized that Athena's meandering path was purposeful. The whinnie chose her path to avoid thickets and anything that would distract her rider.

To their left, the draw climbed up the mountain into a thicker forest that appeared to level out into a tight, but extended, valley that curved toward the northern rim of the tableland. There was no sign of how far it stretched. On their right, toward the summit location of OP Two, large, recent rock falls covered most of the area. Boulders the size of automobiles littered the landscape that would have given them the fastest way up to the high shelf of land. Aliza saw Athena stare up that slope for a moment before angling back to the left.

"What have you got, girl?"

Athena pressed ahead, faster now. Aliza looked over her shoulder and saw the rest of the patrol scrambling up the hill toward the vertical face they'd climbed. None of the whinnies appeared to have any trouble duplicating her feat. Aliza relaxed and let Athena pick up her pace.

As they climbed into the forested area, the intense heat relented and Aliza could feel a cool—well, less hot—breeze on her skin. She wiped a sleeve across her forehead and reached for a canteen on her load-bearing equipment harness—olive drab canvas "H" straps attached to a pistol belt with a metal clasp. It wasn't the most comfortable apparatus she'd ever worn, but it carried canteens, ammunition, her M1911 pistol, and a couple of other pouches with ease.

The water was cool and good, and Aliza drank greedily. As she slipped the canteen back into its container, the rustling of the taller tree-like plants filled the little valley with a peaceful sound. But there was something else on the wind.

"Whoa, girl." Aliza tugged the reins and Athena stopped. Closing her eyes, Aliza put her entire focus on the sensory input from her ears. In the breeze, there was a barely audible trickling sound.

*Water.*

She smiled. *I knew it! All we had to do was search up along this side of the tableland.*

Turning her head slowly, Aliza tried to locate the sound. She tugged Athena in that direction and the big whinnie trotted up the slope and between several copses of trees. In the center of a group of five trees was a small pool only a few feet across. On the uphill side of the pool there was a rock overhang. The water in the pool emerged from underground.

*A spring.*

She followed the flow from the overhang, through the pool, to a narrow stream that flowed for about five meters before it darted back underground. There was no sign that the spring returned to the surface anywhere in their vicinity. A lucky find.

Aliza laughed to herself and shook her head in disbelief. She studied the pool and her eyes grew wide in recognition. Several very familiar and very rare plants blossomed at the edge of the water. She wanted to dismount and see them up close, but she remained in the saddle. There was no way of telling if the water was safe enough for them to—

Athena stepped forward and lapped at the pool for several seconds. Satisfied, the whinnie raised her head and turned back to look at Aliza. Her dark eyes almost glittered. If it could have laughed, she imagined the whinnie would have.

Aliza's mouth fell open. "You knew."

Athena made a purring sound and stepped to the left of the pool and the tiny stream and continued up the valley. Dumbstruck in the saddle, Aliza didn't react until they'd gone twenty meters beyond the spring. She looked back toward the pool and couldn't see it.

"What the hell?" She listened for a moment and could still hear it. The perfectly camouflaged pool wasn't something casually seen or located. A very lucky find.

*No. A deliberate one. They led us here.*

The sound of an approaching whinnie at a fast trot caught her attention, and she turned to see Whittaker riding toward her.

He pointed over at the hidden pool. "Aliza? Did you see that?"

She smiled. "I did. Athena drank from it. They knew it was here."

He shook his head. "I'll be damned."

Aliza brushed her dusty clothes. "Seems that way. What do you want to do?"

Whittaker pointed up the valley. "Follow this around the bend as far as it goes. There has to be another way up to the tableland. If Athena wants us to go that way, we probably should."

Aliza pointed at the radio handset on Whittaker's harness. Unlike Captain Moorefield, he'd chosen to carry the heavy radio himself. "We should report this."

Whittaker grunted and reached for the handset. "I'll try. Line of sight to OP Two has been terrible."

Aliza swept back a lock of her hair the freshening breeze was fluttering across her face. She turned toward the west and saw a low cloud on the—

Not a low cloud. An enormous dust cloud. *They're coming after us.*

"Sergeant Whittaker?"

He paused and looked where she stared. "OP Two, Saber Nine. Over."

A static-filled voice replied. "Saber Nine, OP Two. Be advised enemy attacking in your direction. Saber Six is en route to your position now. Advise you find a way up to the tableland fast. Over."

Whittaker turned back to the curving, narrowing valley. "Negative, OP Two. Relay to Saber Six, we're preparing a hasty defense. Tell him to bust his ass and join us. I'll hang a lantern for him. Out."

"A lantern? It's full daylight?" Aliza asked.

"An expression. I'll post a guide down below to get them up here in a hurry. We've got other things to do right now."

"As in preparing a defense instead of climbing up and over?" Aliza asked. "Isn't that Captain Moorefield's decision?"

"He knows the stakes, Aliza." Whittaker frowned. "They're moving too fast, and we have the advantage of the high ground here. If they get up on the tableland, they won't stop until they roll up everything we have. Our job was to deceive *and delay* the enemy, and that's exactly what we have to do. We hold them here at least until he can slam those stolen vehicles into their flank."

"You're certain?"

Whittaker grinned. "It's what I'd do."

* * *

Whittaker's report was exactly what Bo wanted to hear and his own plan of action crystallized. The immobile gun platform sitting utterly broken in the middle of the trail's tightest section had become a solution, rather than a problem. The craggy rock formations pinning it from either side restricted movement in the immediate area. Leaving the trail to cut a new path up the pass would take a significant investment in time and blood. While their enemy might have the resolve to do so, the trail's blockage could be used to channelize them to wherever Bo wanted them to go.

*Until they get the vehicle out of there, that is.* Which they might very well be able to accomplish, given the larger vehicles they'd seen in reconnaissance. Yanking the broken vehicle out with something more powerful than a handful of whinnies wouldn't be that hard. Bo studied the rocks on either side and smiled.

*Unless it is so jammed that even vehicles can't get it out of the way.*

He grabbed the handset from Sublete and thumb-stabbed the transmit button. "OP Two, relay to Seeker Six. Need their sappers or demo team at the block point to detonate this vehicle and the surrounding rock formations. I want them to collapse the pass completely at this location. Over."

"Saber Six, OP Two. Roger all. TRP set on location and we'll get the sappers moving that direction immediately. Over."

"OP Two, roger that. I'm moving to Saber Nine now," Bo said. He took a quick breath. "Contact Saber Nine for grid coordinates in front of their positions and stand by for contingency Charlie on my call. Saber Six, out."

He handed the handset back to Sublete and nodded at the young man. The young soldier projected confidence. "Ready to move, sir."

Bo pointed at Sublete's mount. "You've ridden him at a full gallop before?"

"A couple of times. A few minutes, tops."

"Then hang on for dear life, son." Bo wheeled Scout to the east and waved at Cook. "When we get to the bottom, dismount and find a vehicle. Leave your whinnie; it'll be fine. We'll mount up and attack to the north, into their flank. Once we blow up the pass, they'll take the bait and commit fully toward our screen. That's when we'll hit them. You'll be the lead vehicle in the attack."

"Yes, sir!" Cook nudged his mount, and the whinnie launched into a trot that quickly became a full gallop across the desert.

"Go, Sublete. I'm right behind you." The RTO and his mount sped after Cook with a good interval between them. Anything they could do to confuse, confound, and slow down the enemy would be the priority. From the upslope side of the collapsed vehicle, Bo heard a group of whinnies approaching.

He didn't wait for them to dismount and prepare the explosives. "C'mon, Scout!" He tapped the whinnie's side gently. "Time to put steel on target."

* * *

Once out of the pass, Bo rode straight for the ragged line of vehicles concealed in the rocks and scrub. Cook was near the center and gestured toward a six-wheeled vehicle with a fat, wide turret on top of its hull. Its two large cannons pointed out over the front windows. They moved slightly from left to right and Bo knew they were already seeing, and tracking, the enemy.

He was already working his feet out of the stirrups and Scout's harness as they slid to a stop. He dismounted the whinnie and saw Scout's triangular head turn his way. The animal's eyes were calm and focused, and despite their frantic pace down the mesa, he appeared to be breathing normally.

"Go home, Scout." Bo turned around and made for the vehicles. The whinnie didn't move. He pointed up the steep skirts of the tableland toward their compound and paddock. "Scout! Go home."

Scout trumpeted softly. The tone was deep and mournful, but the whinnie turned and trotted toward the bottom of the slope and made its way to the north. The other dismounted whinnies followed.

Bo watched them for a second until Specialist Sublete appeared at his shoulder. "Sir, Saber Nine."

"Saber Nine, Six, go," Bo said into the handset.

"Confirm that OpFor regiment is advancing in three echelons. Forward elements are two, I say again, two mechanized infantry battalions. More or less. They're moving toward our position now in a line abreast formation. Third echelon is behind them a couple of klicks or so. They appear to be heavy indirect fire weapons. Not artillery pieces, but with elevated tubes and smaller bores. Probably mortar carriers. How copy?"

Bo clenched and relaxed his jaw. "Good copy. Anything else?"

"We're in a solid defensive position, sir. What are your intentions? Over."

"Counterattack. We'll hit the southernmost echelon first. Either kill them or turn them toward the others. Based on the cloud, I don't think we'll intercept the further echelon until they're on top of your position."

"Looks like that to me, too, sir. We'll hold the second echelon provided their artillery isn't accurate." Whittaker paused. "If it is, we've got some secondary positions identified."

*It will have to do.*

Cook pointed at the big vehicle. "Sir, you're in this one. Sublete is on the next vehicle over."

Bo nodded and turned to Sublete. "Flag me down if the shit hits the fan."

"Yes, sir," Sublete replied and went to his vehicle.

"You've got Private Jackson and Private Cleric onboard this one, sir. It's rough around the edges but can hammer armor from what the indigs tell us." Cook moved toward the vehicle and kept talking. "There's a hatch up top. You'll probably want to use it: old school everything in this bucket."

"Thanks, Cook. Good hunting," Bo said and scrambled up onto the quiet vehicle using rungs on the right rear of the vehicle's hull. He crossed over the engine deck and stepped easily onto the turret. An oval hatch in the center of the turret beckoned. He stooped and swung his legs down, putting his body halfway into the turret. He felt around with his soles and found a small shelf where he could stand. *Some things are the same wherever you go.* The amount of bodily exposure while standing in the hatch reminded him of the M1 Abrams.

There was a rudimentary headset hanging on the lip of the hatch. He slipped it over his head and heard the two soldiers talking over the crew intercom.

"Crew report," Bo said.

"Driver ready, sir," Jackson replied.

"Gunner ready, sir," Cleric said. "I'm below you and to your left. Jackson is in the hull. We have eighty rounds aboard and we're ready to go."

Bo smiled. *Not bad for making it up as we go.*

"Standby for ignition short count," Bo called. "We have no radios with the others, correct?"

"Not really, sir. Some data sharing at my console, but direct comms are inoperable," Cleric said. "Gotta do it the old-fashioned way."

"Roger that," Bo replied. *Let's hope everyone remembers hand and arm signals.*

He stood in the hatch and looked in both directions. Every vehicle had at least one crew member looking his way. He waved the signal for "attention" and followed it with the sign for "prepare to move." As he made the circular motion, he called to Jackson. "Start in three, two, one."

The vehicle growled to life under him. The other vehicles seemed to answer with their own roars and turbine-screams. Bo held both arms out to his sides indicating a line formation and ensured that all the crews saw him. He gave them the signal to move forward, and the line rumbled into the scrub and picked up speed.

"What can you see, Cleric?"

"It's got a decent thermal type sight, sir. I can see the first battalion now. We're coming in on their flank."

Bo kept his eyes on the formation. He pumped his fist into the sky several times. "Floor it, Jackson! As soon as we're in range, Cleric, pick your targets and start firing."

"Yes, sir!" both men answered in unison.

The vehicle picked up speed and bounced across the rocky terrain. Bo grabbed at the edge of the hatch for safety and wished there was any type of machine gun mount there to hold on to. His time aboard the Abrams, with its .50 caliber machine gun mount on the commander's hatch, had spoiled him.

Cleric fired, the twin cannons discharging a half second apart. What rounds they fired Bo could not track as there was no tracer element. However, when they impacted the side of a similar vehicle in the attacking column, the results were spectacular. Along the line, Bo watched his vehicles fire and adjust into the marching battalion. The attackers never had a chance.

"Hell, yeah!" Cleric yelled over the intercom. The turret swiveled to the right and fired again. Another vehicle, this one a dune buggy-thing full of infantry, detonated in a bright orange fireball. "They've gotta be seven hundred meters away!"

Bo agreed based on what he could see. As the surprise effect waned, the enemy formation did not veer off to flee, but instead turned into the approaching Lost Soldier formation for a counterattack. From his position at the center of the line, Bo saw the edges starting to slow and push his formation into a vee shape. He flagged down the vehicles on the extreme left as Cleric kept up a steady rate of fire, locating, ranging, and engaging one target after another. The line sped up and closed with the surprised enemy.

As the distance between the formations closed, the firefight began in earnest. One of Bo's vehicles on the right side of the line exploded as they charged into the enemy flank. They hit another on his left, which heeled to a stop, smoking sullenly. But his attack kept moving forward and putting rounds downrange. Accurate rounds, whereas a great deal of the J'Stull shots went wild. *Because it must be just like the locals told us,* Bo thought with a nod at the absent indigs: *almost none of the OpFor have any significant training.* In fact, if the intel was as correct as it seemed to be, most were just strong-arm enforcers.

Cleric fired again and again. Dust and smoke obscured more and more of the enemy formation. Bo frantically signaled his line to slow down, but they kept charging forward into the cloud. One second, Bo could see the battlefield and the next, the white and brown cloud encircled them. A flash of movement caught his eye, and he spun to see an enemy vehicle with a wide-bored gun tube pointed in his direction.

"Contact left!" he called.

Cleric swung the turret hard left as Jackson yanked the vehicle in the opposite direction. Bo lost his grip on the hatch ring. One moment he was standing in the hatch; the next, the vehicle's lurch sent him skittering across the top of the vehicle. He slid off its side toward the rocky ground two meters below.

*Shit!*

He hit the ground and instinctively rolled away from his vehicle's wheels. Pain swam in from every limb and almost every part of his torso. Eyes closed and face pressed into the desert floor, Bo quickly evaluated his body by feel. Nothing was broken, but he'd have a damned hard time moving as he recovered from the impact.

He rolled over and sat up. The dust and smoke continued to swirl around him, and the sound of the battle seemed more distant to his left and right than in his immediate position.

*We cut right through them.*

Bo stood and patted his holster; his pistol was missing. He searched the ground nearby but didn't see the weapon. A round of some type whistled through the air above his head. Scared into action, he dashed forward to a rock outcropping only a meter high and flung himself behind it. He pushed up close to the rock and peered over its jagged edges.

There was nothing worth seeing in the nearby dust and smoke. Vehicles were burning. The sound of weapons firing and vehicles moving had almost faded to nothing. As elated as he was that the first stage of the attack had gone so well, Bo realized he was alone and unarmed amid an enemy formation's route of march. He slumped against the rock, pressing his face against the warm, rough stone. His thoughts were a sudden whirl of recollected survival skills, escape and evasion techniques, and how to find his way back to the tableland. The intense heat of R'Bak's stars hammered through the dust, but he didn't move. Instead, he took a deep breath, and with his head throbbing, sighed dejectedly.

*Well, shit.*

\* \* \* \* \*

# Chapter Eight

No sooner had the captured vehicles attacked when the first rounds of indirect fire fell across Saber Nine's position on the high ground at the back of the draw. Aliza, with Sergeant Whittaker behind a rock outcropping, had a good view of their entire defensive front. The first rounds fell in the vicinity of the upper positions from which riflemen were laying down fire over and across the rest of the patrol. Shrapnel from the enemy shells ricocheted off the rock walls and caused little damage. Others missed their position entirely. A few made it to the more exposed positions at the top of the wall and tore them to bits.

As soon as the first barrage ended, Whittaker leapt off the front of their position to gather the wounded. His eyes looked back and caught hers as he dragged one soldier away from the forward positions; his glance was both a question and a summons. She jumped into action and helped the sergeant.

Working at different points along their line, they dragged three of the injured to more protected positions, finishing just as the second barrage fell. The enemy had improved their targeting, and the shells dropped with greater accuracy but still had little effect.

As the interval between explosions slowed, Aliza saw Sergeant Whittaker jump up from cover. As he began sprinting in her direction, a mortar round exploded ten meters behind him along the top of the escarpment.

Time seemed to slow. She saw, in terrible detail, shrapnel tear through his right leg as he ran. His next step with the left leg was fine, but as his right leg went forward to meet the ground again, it buckled and he crumpled to the ground, his shocked and anguished face just ten meters from hers. He panted, blinked—and another round detonated almost on top of him, flinging him in her direction.

Before he'd even stopped tumbling, Aliza dropped her pistol atop the rock and bounded toward him. Adrenaline flowing, she grabbed him by the shoulders and dragged him backward, to her position. More rounds rushed down, sent shrapnel sleeting. It was as if she could feel every fragment passing through the surrounding sky. One passed close enough that she felt it tug on her hair. Another missed penetrating her left boot by a fraction.

Halfway to the outcrop, she looked down at Whittaker as she strained backward, her rush of adrenaline almost expended. His eyes were closed, and his mouth was a tight, white line. Then his eyes opened, locked onto hers for a moment, and then squeezed shut again. Blood seeped from innumerable wounds and turned his olive drab fatigues a slick, wet black.

She screamed before she had even registered the frustration and rage which sent the violent sound out of her. Tears blurred her vision as she pulled Whittaker into cover and collapsed by his side. Lungs burning with the effort, she blinked away her tears and reached for Whittaker's first aid compress. His right hand touched hers, and she stopped.

"It's okay, Aliza," he wheezed. His eyes were bright and clear. Where there had been pain across his wrinkled face there was now acceptance, almost peace. "It's okay. I lived…twice. Don't mind dying twice. Not for—"

She took his hand, squeezed it. "Don't…don't leave me. Please!"

Whittaker smiled and there was a beauty to it she'd never imagined. She took his hand in both of hers. His grip weakened, failed, and his gaze became a sightless stare over her shoulder into the cloudless sky.

She lowered her face to her hands and cried. As she did, Aliza realized her tears were not just for Sergeant Whittaker, but for her family, her friends, and Ben Mazza. They were tears she'd never shed. They came with a force that surprised her, and in her grief, there was something new. In the months since Dachau—months a century and a half in the past—she'd experienced rage and frustration tinged with tiny glimpses of hope and love. Instead of clinging to those glimpses, she'd embraced the anger, tried to let it fuel her.

But tears? They were new. She could feel what they meant, what they were telling her: it was time to let them go. As she cradled Whittaker's lifeless hand in hers, a warm trickle of blood ran down across her wrist and into the crease of where her slender hand clutched the hard, broad palm of the dead sergeant. Almost calmly, she realized her right arm was bleeding from the muscles in her forearm. The pain was considerable and getting worse by the second. She also realized the barrage was over.

Aliza stood, started unevenly toward the most heavily shelled positions, determined to do exactly what she and Whittaker had done before. There was risk of course, and they might all be trapped in a future none of them wanted, but they were here and the only way they'd ever see Earth again was to take care of each other.

And that, she decided as she scrambled forward, was better than rage and frustration.

\* \* \*

Bo took off his uniform blouse and draped it over his head and shoulders. The sounds of the attack intensified in the north. Every report sent a bolt of pain through his head. As much as he wanted to follow it, he was alone and there were still enemy vehicles and personnel surrounding his position. Either they would retreat or move to re-consolidate with their surviving forces. It was a matter of time. Without a weapon, transportation, or water, Bo knew his best choice was to stay put even as the clouds of failure swirled through his mind. It hadn't been a perfect plan, but he'd been confident in its success.

*It could be succeeding. You're just stuck out here because you fell off your fucking mount, Bo.*

On cue, Sharron's words came to mind. *You always think things rely on you. You're so self-centered sometimes I can't even believe it. All I wanted was for you to care about me. About us. You cared more about things you thought had gone wrong or that slighted you somehow. My life isn't about you, Bo. Not anymore.*

He shook his head and strained to peer over the top of his rock-strewn position. Movement caught his eye in both directions. There was no way he could move. Not for a while at least. He settled back against the rock and hung his head to his chest in resignation. The breeze freshened slightly in his face and he raised his eyes enough that he saw his missing boonie hat caught in a cactus-like plant a few meters away. He crawled forward and reached for the hat—

The sound of several rifles firing nearby rang out. Bo flinched away from the hat even as his brain told him they weren't firing at him. He leaned forward and snatched the hat away from the plant and heard a deep, throaty roar. A whinnie charged directly toward him at full gallop.

*Not just any whinnie.* Bo grinned and got up to a low crouch. He slapped the hat on his head and worked his arms through the sleeves of his blouse. There wasn't time to finish buttoning it up before Scout reared up and bounced to a stop in front of him.

As Scout settled in front of Bo, streaks of dark purplish blood streamed from several wounds on the whinnie's side. Bo stood and went to him. The bullet holes were small, and he counted ten of them on the right side of Scout's neck. His first impulse was to grab his field dressing and tear the package open to press it against the worst of the wounds.

Scout hooted and slammed Bo's shoulder with his triangular jaw. The whinnie jerked its chin toward the saddle and hooted again, this time much deeper.

*He wants me to get aboard.*

"You sure, buddy?"

Scout made the deep purring sound and then shook his head and body, not unlike a dog trying to dry itself after a dip in a lake.

*He's telling you he's okay, Bo. He's shaking it off.*

*My God, we're communicating.*

Rounds impacted nearby, but Scout held his ground. A gun-shy mount would have bolted, but Scout stood resolute. Bo climbed aboard and patted Scout's left forward shoulder, the one opposite of the wounds. "We can do this, buddy. Get me to Athena and the others."

Scout took off again, this time back to the east and the distant tableland. From the very first time he'd galloped a horse at fourteen, Bo learned a valuable lesson. Moving that fast astride an animal, especially one built for speed, distorted time and distance. On the farm, he'd intended to only ride his first horse, Maverick, for two minutes at a gallop before slowing down. He'd judged that he could ride to the far posts of the main pasture and back in that timeframe. When it had taken almost double that time, and Maverick was surly at him for a few days afterward, Bo had realized what had happened. A full-out gallop took a lot of energy for a horse, especially when they weren't used to running like that. Aboard Scout, he kept wanting to hold the big animal back, but Scout never relented. Though it seemed impossible, as Bo hunched over the saddle to be more aerodynamic, he thought the whinnie kept a pace far faster than they'd done on the tableland.

"Atta boy, Scout!" Bo called as they raced across the scrub. Branches tore at his boots and pants, but Bo didn't care. His eyes remained locked on the high plateau. He turned once when the dust and smoke started to thin, saw the second enemy echelon approaching a draw that appeared to be where Whittaker and the others had prepared their defense. In that same direction but in the middle distance, Bo saw a pale whinnie standing and looking toward them. He didn't immediately recognize the mount or its rider but headed toward them.

Less than a minute later, Scout skidded to a stop next to Private Morton, a gangly kid from New York with shockingly red hair. Bo smiled; Whittaker had indeed hung out a fire-topped lantern for him.

"Captain Moorefield? They reported you dead," Morton blurted.

"Not yet." Bo smiled. "Get us to Sergeant Whittaker and the others."

The redhead grinned and tugged his mount up the trail. "Follow me, sir."

They bounced up the trail for a minute, and the draw came into view. An escarpment spanned the back of it like a dried-up waterfall. About five meters tall, the wall it created was imposing and perfect for defense. At the top of the wall, and atop the nearly sheer valley slopes flanking it, Bo saw the soldiers of Sections Three and Four manning hasty defensive positions. He smiled to himself. Whittaker had chosen those parts of the high ground with good observation and fields of fire. The experienced sergeant had also placed firing teams above them on the rocks for air defense and better geometry for the attacking force at the valley's mouth. The position was utterly defensible despite the dust and smoke swirling about them from the enemy's indirect fire attempts.

*This might just work.*

Whittaker had positioned the sections of four in multiple locations. Two were on the rocks above the tight valley in prone positions behind cover. They appeared to be in good shape as they opened fire. Bo couldn't see the enemy infantry, but he could hear them screaming as they ran up the draw.

Several explosions drowned out the sound of battle for a few seconds. The OpFor's indirect fire weapons weren't dropping accurate fire on the position. They couldn't see it from their position out in the valley and with no forward observer to actually plot and correct their firing solutions, they were firing blind and hoping to have some, if any, effect.

*It's meant to deplete us. Harass us. Rattle us enough that their infantry rolls all over us.*

*Not this time.*

They kept moving toward the position as a new barrage of indirect fire came down. This time the fire was more accurate. Soldiers scattered in all directions as the small, powerful explosions rocked the draw. Morton had frozen in the saddle of his mount. Bo bounded Scout around the shocked pair and raced into the position as the enemy infantry came into view at the wall below.

\* \* \*

The artillery fire ended abruptly, and she heard the forward positions engage the infantry again as she stood. A whinnie clambered down from the rocks above. She recognized the rider and felt fresh tears fall on her cheeks as he approached at a gallop. Moorefield dismounted his whinnie and ran toward her. Words failed her and all she could do was shake her head. The young captain knelt by the body of Whittaker and touched his neck. Finding no pulse, he simply put his hand on the sergeant's shoulder and squeezed. She couldn't see his face under the brim of his floppy hat, but she felt his grief. The *crack!* of a single rifle fired from the points above them snapped both of their heads back to the wall at the mouth of the tiny valley.

He stood and looked at her. "You're in charge here, Aliza. Sergeant Cook is your platoon sergeant. I'm taking Stewart with me. Move everyone who can fire into position behind cover in case any of them get up here. Tell them to shoot whatever they can see and keep shooting until we come across the valley. Don't hit us."

"What are you doing?"

He smiled grimly. "Sounding the charge."

She blinked. "You're what?"

He pointed. "The whinnies can make it down the slope with us on their backs. We just have to hold on and trust them not to dump us. We'll surprise the infantry and drive them toward our vehicles. You pin them down, and we'll smoke them out."

"But that's crazy!"

"Not really." He turned back to her. "We have the advantage of moving downhill. With speed and as much firepower as we can pour on them, we can pin their infantry between us and our vehicles down there. If the mortars are ready, we can rain steel on their heads and push their regiment back long enough so we can escape up the tableland and evacuate Camp Stark."

There was a clinical logic to his thinking. Before she noticed it, she was nodding.

"You want us to stay here and harass the infantry below. Hold them in place for your charge to sweep them across to us, yes?"

"Precisely. Can you do that?"

She felt a genuine smile cross her face. "If you'd said to sit still and wait for rescue, I would have said no. We'll hold them down, Bo. Go sound your charge."

He grinned at her and reached down to Whittaker's radio. He hesitated for a moment, grabbed and holstered the fallen sergeant's pistol, and then picked up the handset. "Saber Six Romeo, Saber Six. You read me?"

"Holy shit, sir! We thought you were dead," Sublete replied.

"Alive and kicking," Bo replied. "I want you moving toward the valley entrance. Slowly. We'll scare up the infantry in your direction with a little cavalry charge. When you see that, you call for contingency Charlie. My authority. Tell the vehicle commanders to lift and shift their fire until we find cover and then let anything escaping to the west have it. Over."

"Roger, Saber Six. Good copy. Give 'em hell."

Bo dropped the radio handset and turned, shouting orders to all the riders. From up the valley, the whinnies ran back to the soldiers and knelt to be mounted. Something seemed off and after a second of staring wide-eyed, she could see there were more whinnies than riders. At least twenty had no saddles on their strong backs. They'd come with the herd.

*To charge our common enemy.*

The electricity of the thought spurred her to action. "Sergeant Cook!"

He looked over at her. "Yes, ma'am?"

"Gather the wounded. Everyone that can shoot gets in position behind these outcroppings. If we've got a few more who can get up on the high ground, get them up there. We don't have much time to lay down fire for the charge." She didn't wait for a response. Instead, she spun and reached down for Whittaker's radio, remembering their radio procedures by heart. "OP Two, Saber Nine, update on the mortars. Over."

There was no response. She snorted. "Then we'll just hope they get in position soon."

She grabbed Whittaker's M14 and spare magazines from his load-bearing equipment. The peace on his pale face had settled as slight creases and deeper wrinkles, like an old man who had fallen deep asleep in a hammock. She smiled and placed her hand on his. "Let's hope you're right about dying twice, my friend. Thank you. I will see you soon, but not today. Not if I can help it."

No tears came, which surprised her. There would be time for more of them, but it would not be now. She stood, cradled the rifle at what the soldiers called the low ready and ran forward toward the wall. She took up a firing position and saw the enemy infantry dismounting their vehicles and rushing toward the opening.

A sharp whistle from above caught her attention, and she spun to the right. Atop the rocks and back from the upper firing positions, she saw Bo and the others. He waved at her, and she checked the soldiers to her right and left and those at the other outcroppings. She gave him a thumbs-up and turned to the soldiers under her unlikely command. It was time to do what she hadn't been able do for Ben Mazza and the others.

"Open fire!"

\* \* \*

As Aliza's defensive positions rained direct fire on the infantry below, Bo turned to Sergeant Stewart halfway down the poised line of whinnies. The ones without riders surprised him, but he said nothing. Scout and the others evidently understood the stakes and, given their intelligence and disposition, they had brought the rest of the herd into the fray. The wounds on Scout's neck seeped blood, but there was no sign that the whinnie was in pain or even distracted by them. Several others had more serious wounds yet stood alongside the others on the upper surface of the eastern wall.

"We'll sweep downhill like a swinging door," Bo said. "Stewart, your side stays pinned close to the bottom of the wall as we go across. This end will sweep out, all the way toward the enemy vehicles. Move as quickly as you can. The whinnies will bound down these rocks faster than anything you've ever seen. Just hold on for dear life until you reach the floor of the draw. Once you're there, commence firing and stay in your lane. Once we hit the enemy flank, all hell will break loose. Push them south toward our vehicles. They will eventually regroup. When they do and start to return fire, find cover. Until then, watch out for each other and good hunting."

The soldiers all nodded, and their faces were more serious than he'd ever seen. Gone were any expressions of bored indifference or guarded resentment. Some of their friends lay wounded below them. A few were dead. They all knew the cost and there was nothing in their present demeanor to suggest they would shy away from it. Still, he sensed trepidation.

Bo smiled, made sure his nod was one of casual, and therefore absolute, confidence. "It'll work, guys. The 20th Maine did the same thing at Gettysburg. Won the field and likely the whole damned war that day. Just stay in line and keep firing."

Stewart waved a hand. "Sir?"

"What is it, Stewart?"

The sergeant slowly smiled. "Was just wishing we had a bugler. You know? To sound the fucking charge?"

The soldiers laughed together and their tension broke.

Bo waved one last time to Aliza. "Hell," he said loudly, "who needs a damned bugle?" He nudged Scout forward and shouted, "Charge!"

Around him, the soldiers and the whinnies raised their faces in a matching cry and raced down the hill together, straight toward the flank of the J'Stull infantry.

"Go, Scout! I'm with you." Bo wrapped the reins around his hands and squeezed the whinnie tightly with his legs. Scout bounced between two rocks and then shot downhill in a series of bounds that took Bo's breath away. The last leap took them to mostly level ground. Through the brush on both sides, he saw the line was intact and starting to swing. From his position near the far end, he saw the unmounted whinnies charging forward of the line.

Beneath him, Scout roared. It was a sound he'd never heard from any of the whinnies. The ones charging forward slowed to stay in formation, to keep with the line as it pivoted. They charged over a slight rise and descended to the flatland of the draw and toward the loosely arrayed enemy infantry.

The surprise was complete. Intent on finding a way up to silence the stiff fire from Aliza's defenders and to reach the tableland higher up, the enemy hadn't seen or heard the whinnies coming. Turning to discover a charging line of cavalrymen and ferocious animals bearing down upon them, the enemy infantry panicked and ran. They scattered, some falling back toward their vehicles but most simply fleeing away from the charging whinnies. If any of them realized that the direction of the charge was actually herding them south of the attacking vehicle column, there was no sign of it.

In seconds, Bo and the others were among them. Pistol in hand, Bo kept hold of the reins with his left and fired with his right. Some of the enemy stood their ground only to be cut down by weapons, or in more terrifying ways by the whinnies. A man Bo hadn't seen appeared on his left side. Before he could pivot with his weapon, Scout darted that direction without breaking stride. He snapped his jaws, and the man fell to the ground, both hands amputated in a spray of blood.

*Holy shit!*

"Go, Scout! Get 'em, big guy!" Bo yelled. It felt good enough that he screamed from his diaphragm. The others joined him, and the whinnies roared. The enemy infantry's panic became absolute. Those who had fled without any initial direction now raced for the imagined protection of their vehicles.

The gun platforms on the enemy carriers opened fire. Bo and the riders leaned forward to lower their profiles as they charged. A whinnie on his right went down with a howl. He heard a *smack* as a bullet missed his left leg and tore a gash in Scout's hide. The big whinnie roared again, and Bo expected him to bolt further forward when he dashed hard left instead. The entire line moved that way without a command and ran east toward the sheer, soaring sides of the tableland.

"Scout! What are you doing?" Bo tugged the reins hard to the right, but Scout wouldn't change course. "Scout! You're going the wrong—"

*WHUMP! WHUMP!*

Bo whipped his head to the right and saw a series of explosions around the enemy vehicles as mortar rounds fell in and among them.

Contingency Charlie was on time and on target. And was very close—or would have been, had Scout and the other whinnies not heard and understood the significance of the incoming mortar rounds.

Between the withering barrage, the captured vehicles roaring out of the south, and the line of whinnies that had slowed and stopped just beyond the mortars' beaten zone, the enemy infantry threw down their weapons and fled west. Still in a line abreast formation, they faced as one into the rising dust cloud of explosions and watched the steel rain fall.

The barrage hammered down for several minutes, completely obscuring any view to the west. A trooper from third section appeared out of the thin smoke from the direction of the wall, the unit's radio on his shoulder. "Sir! Sir! We've got comms again!"

Bo reached for the handset. "OP Two, Saber Six. Relay to the mortars cease fire. I say again, cease fire. Over."

"OP Two, roger, out."

A few more rounds moaned through the sky above them, chasing after the dim shapes of the J'Stull vehicles, and exploded on impact among them. Silence fell across the valley. Bo pressed the handset again.

"Saber Nine, Saber Six. SITREP, over."

Aliza's voice came back a little shaken, but steady. "Saber Six, we took more casualties, Bo, but we're okay."

"Roger, we'll be back there soon." He glanced at Stewart. "Post an OP and observe them. See if there are survivors and such. Let them collect their dead and wounded. If they mass forces or start any movement east of their line, I want to know about it."

"Yes, sir," Stewart replied. "On it."

"Make it happen," Bo said. He watched with pride as the young sergeant raced back toward the mouth of the valley with a section of four riders.

"Saber Six, OP Two with a relay from Starkpatch, over."

"Send it, OP Two."

"Starkpatch relays Glass Palace. All enemy elements withdrawing at speed. Evacuation of Camp Stark delayed pending further observation of OpFor movement. Major Murphy sends outstanding work. Orders are for you to maintain reconnaissance and prepare for next phase. How copy? Over."

Bo grinned and wiped his chin with a sleeve. "Good copy. We'll start extraction immediately. I'm positioning OP One forward again to observe the enemy here. I want you to move to the mortar platoon to augment their security. Over."

"Roger, Saber Six. Displacing now. Will report from mortar position. OP Two, out."

He passed the handset back to the trooper and put his hands on his hips for a moment and then thought better of it. There wasn't time to relax.

"Back to the wall. Good job, troopers. Move out!"

* * * * *

# Chapter Nine

The scene at the top of the wall was not what Bo expected. Aliza and the others had the wounded ready for evacuation. Those who could walk moved up the slope toward the top of the tableland where a truck-become-ambulance was standing by. Those who could not walk were carried atop the whinnies. The remaining soldiers silently collected the dead and secured their weapons and equipment.

Aliza saw Bo approach and walked in his direction. "Six dead. Fourteen wounded. Only two seriously. We're moving them up to the rim as quickly as we can. Lieutenant Meehan has vehicles standing by to recover us."

Bo nodded. "Anything else?"

"There's a potable spring just up the draw. The way it flows back underground suggests there might be a cave system here. Maybe an aquifer, too. That could be useful during the Sear," Aliza said. She tucked an errant lock of hair behind one ear and kept talking. "There are some medicinals at the spring. We've identified several species including *londau'd* and *ogh-ul*. They are perennials, but extremely rare. Rare enough that when the actual Harvesters arrive, they are almost certain to know to come here in search of them. And I think there are more nearby."

"Get what you can, Aliza," Bo replied. "But you have to hurry. If the J'Stull don't keep running, they'll soon realize that we've blocked the fastest ways up to the tableland. If they can, they'll come after us again. We'll be ready for that, but if they do, they've seen our positions and know the kind of force and tactics they'll need. So, we've got to be gone if and when they get here."

Aliza sighed and a faint smile crossed her lips. "I've been wishing to not be here since I woke."

He squinted at her. "But you feel differently now?"

She nodded. "It's not something I can explain."

For a moment, Bo wanted to push the subject, but something held him back. "Would you take me to the spring and show me the medicinals? You're better versed on them than I am. I wouldn't know what to look for if it was sprouting right in front of me."

She grinned. "It's right over there."

Bo slid off Scout and absently brushed the dust and dirt from his pants before falling into step alongside the young brunette. They walked in silence. With a fresh breeze rustling the vegetation and the wind pushing the smells of battle away from them, the early afternoon was almost pleasant.

The tiny pool of water looked cool and inviting. They stopped and Bo knelt by the water's edge and studied the clear liquid and the various multi-colored and very alien-looking plants there. "And we're sure it's safe to drink?"

"Athena drank from it with no ill effects," Aliza replied. "The whinnies have always shied away from the water sources we determined to be bad. It bodes well for this one."

"That's still taking an awful risk, Aliza."

She knelt beside him, stuck both hands into the water and made a reservoir with her palms. Before he could stop her, she brought her hands to her face and said, *"L'Chaim!"*

"What did you just do?"

Aliza made a satisfied sound and laughed. "I took your risks for you, Bo. Sometimes the greatest risk is to take none."

He reached out and took her hand. When she didn't flinch away, he smiled at her. "That's not something I want you to do for me, Aliza. What does that mean? *L'Chaim?*"

"'To life.'" Her smile slipped away. "Every moment you have it is a moment worth celebrating."

"I suppose so," Bo said. He wanted to stare into her eyes, but he glanced away.

When she spoke again, her voice was faint, tentative. "Sergeant Whittaker said you needed to find your heart, Bo. What did he mean?"

Bo chuckled and shook his head as he brought his eyes back to hers. "None of us started this new future with a blank slate. Some of us have carried more pain than any human should carry."

"Maybe there's a way past that pain?" She squeezed his hand, and he returned the gesture.

He looked at her for a long moment. "I can't even imagine what you went through, Aliza."

"You won't have to." She smiled. "This life will differ from our old ones."

Bo chuckled. "I haven't looked at it that way."

"Whittaker said—" a tremor of grief passed across her features "—he said that dying twice was worth it because he lived twice. I think I know what he meant. Living again makes all of this new pain worth it. Particularly because we can use our past to show us how to live better now, rather than allow it to define us all over again." She frowned slightly but was also smiling. "Does that make sense to you?"

"It does."

"I know we're here for a reason and on this mission for a reason." Aliza took a breath. "But I think we're supposed to do much more than hold this ground. We might not be obligated to complete the work, but we cannot abandon it. At least that's what the Talmud says."

"That ain't exactly my department." Bo smiled at her. "I agree that we're part of something much bigger than just us. But I think you're right. To achieve anything, we have to be here for each other."

She smiled, and it captivated him. Aliza Turan was as beautiful as she was genuine and resilient. He'd been very wrong about her.

His heart hammered in his chest when she asked, "So assuming we do not have to flee and keep fleeing—something with which my ancestors were quite familiar—what do we do next?"

Bo tried to force himself to focus on the larger mission. "Two things. One, we really need to understand the whinnies and just how smart they are. Allies out here are scarce, and we haven't even scratched the surface of what they are capable of. Two? One of my lieutenants used to say the simple things were always hard and the hard things were always simple. I think in this case he's right." *About more things than one.*

"What do you mean, Bo?" Aliza squinted at him.

He looked at her but heard Sharron saying the words that, had she been here, he might now have said to her: *I've found someone else who is everything you are not. I can't help but wonder if I'd met them first would I ever have married you? I settled for you, and I was wrong. I've found someone who'll be here for me. You never were. They'll love me in a way you never could.*

Bo looked down and opened the slanted pocket on his uniform blouse. He removed the yellowed paper from its plastic bag and, without unfolding it, slowly tore it into thin strips and then into tiny squares. He scattered them into the freshening wind.

*I can't carry the past anymore. The future is too important. Goodbye, Sharron.* Bo took a long breath and exhaled slowly.

Aliza put a hand on his arm. "What was that?"

"The letter my ex-wife sent to tell me it was over. I opened it the morning the Ktor snagged me. They kept it and made sure I had it."

Her face twisted in a question. "Why would they do such a thing? Surely they read and understood it."

"Maybe." Bo shrugged. "Maybe they thought it would anchor me to who I was or to whatever they had planned for all of us. Or to focus my resentment and anger at her, even more than at them. Either way, I'm done with that."

She smiled again and rolled her left elbow outward, revealing the blue numbers on her smooth inner forearm. "I can't get rid of this so easily."

"It doesn't matter." He looked down at her. One hand traced the line of her jaw and she did not flinch away. Her eyes were dark brown, almost black, yet very bright. So bright that, like mirrors, he saw himself in them, and something far greater, besides. "Like you said, our past doesn't define us, Aliza. We don't have the time to even give it another moment's thought."

She nodded. "Because this isn't over." Aliza stared into his eyes. "It hasn't really started, has it?"

"Not at all. They're coming for us, Aliza. Maybe not today or tomorrow, but they're coming. So, if we want this second chance at life, we have to be ready for them. For anything, really. Even the things we never thought would happen again. There's too much at stake now. Like you said, we might not be obligated to this unexpected future, but we damned sure can't abandon it."

\* \* \* \* \*

# ABOUT THE AUTHOR

Kevin Ikenberry is a life-long space geek and retired Army officer. A former manager of the world-renowned U.S. Space Camp program and space operations officer, Kevin has a broad background in space and space science education. His 2016 debut science fiction novel *Sleeper Protocol* was a Finalist for the Colorado Book Award and was heralded as "an emotionally powerful debut" by *Publisher's Weekly*. Kevin is the author of the military science fiction / thriller novels *Runs In The Family*, *Vendetta Protocol*, and *Super-Sync*. Kevin is a core author in the Four Horsemen Universe where his novels include *Peacemaker, Honor The Threat, Stand Or Fall, Deathangel,* and *Redacted Affairs* (with Kevin Steverson). He is an Active Member of SFWA, and a member of International Thriller Writers. He lives in Colorado with his family – his home is seldom a boring place.

\* \* \* \* \*

# The Caine Riordan Universe

The Caine Riordan series and Terran Republic universe deliver gritty yet doggedly optimistic hard scifi in a world that is a believable and embattled successor to our own. For those who are not familiar with the series' hallmark blend of exploration, alien encounters, intrigue, and action, you can find them all right here:

The **Caine Riordan** series
(Baen Books)
*Fire with Fire*
*Trial by Fire*
*Raising Caine*
*Caine's Mutiny*
*Marque of Caine*
*Endangered Species* (forthcoming)
*Protected Species* (forthcoming)
*Triage* (forthcoming, with Eric Flint)

The **Murphy's Lawless** series
*Shakes*
*Obligations*
*Man-Eater* (coming April 20, 2020)

Other works in the **Terran Republic** universe
*Lost Signals* (Ring of Fire Press)

Since that list includes a winner of the Compton Crook Award, four Nebula finalists, and two Dragon finalists, they're not hard to find. Just go wherever books are sold. Want to learn more about the Caine Riordan series? Easy. Contact any of the publishers, or you can reach out to me at contact@charlesegannon.com.

Want to see more of what's going on in the Terran Republic universe? Check out http://www.charlesegannon.com for exclusive written and visual content.

And if you decide you don't want to miss a single new release or announcement, then go to http://charlesegannon.com/wp/sign-up/ to join the all-inclusive mailing list for sneak peeks, special offers, and features you won't see anywhere else.

And most important of all...welcome aboard; we're glad you're here!

The following is an
**Excerpt from Book One of the Revelations Cycle:**

# Cartwright's Cavaliers

---

# Mark Wandrey

Available Now from Seventh Seal Press

eBook, Paperback, and Audio Book

### Excerpt from "Cartwright's Cavaliers:"

The last two operational tanks were trapped on their chosen path. Faced with destroyed vehicles front and back, they cut sideways to the edge of the dry river bed they'd been moving along and found several large boulders to maneuver around that allowed them to present a hull-down defensive position. Their troopers rallied on that position. It was starting to look like they'd dig in when Phoenix 1 screamed over and strafed them with dual streams of railgun rounds. A split second later, Phoenix 2 followed on a parallel path. Jim was just cheering the air attack when he saw it. The sixth damned tank, and it was a heavy.

"I got that last tank," Jim said over the command net.

"Observe and stand by," Murdock said.

"We'll have these in hand shortly," Buddha agreed, his transmission interspersed with the thudding of his CASPer firing its magnet accelerator. "We can be there in a few minutes."

Jim examined his battlespace. The tank was massive. It had to be one of the fusion-powered beasts he'd read about. Which meant shields and energy weapons. It was heading down the same gap the APC had taken, so it was heading toward Second Squad, and fast.

"Shit," he said.

"Jim," Hargrave said, "we're in position. What are you doing?"

"Leading," Jim said as he jumped out from the rock wall.

\* \* \* \* \*

Get "Cartwright's Cavaliers" now at:
https://www.amazon.com/dp/B01MRZKM95

Find out more about Mark Wandrey and the Four Horsemen Universe at:

https://chriskennedypublishing.com/the-four-horsemen-books/

\* \* \* \* \*

The following is an
**Excerpt from Book One of the Salvage Title Trilogy:**

# Salvage Title

_____

# Kevin Steverson

Available Now from Theogony Books

eBook, Paperback, and Audio Book

### Excerpt from "Salvage Title:"

The first thing Clip did was get power to the door and the access panel. Two of his power cells did the trick once he had them wired to the container. He then pulled out his slate and connected it. It lit up, and his fingers flew across it. It took him a few minutes to establish a link, then he programmed it to search for the combination to the access panel.

"Is it from a human ship?" Harmon asked, curious.

"I don't think so, but it doesn't matter; ones and zeros are still ones and zeros when it comes to computers. It's universal. I mean, there are some things you have to know to get other races' computers to run right, but it's not that hard," Clip said.

Harmon shook his head. *Riiigghht,* he thought. He knew better. Clip's intelligence test results were completely off the charts. Clip opted to go to work at Rinto's right after secondary school because there was nothing for him to learn at the colleges and universities on either Tretra or Joth. He could have received academic scholarships for advanced degrees on a number of nearby systems. He could have even gone all the way to Earth and attended the University of Georgia if he wanted. The problem was getting there. The schools would have provided free tuition if he could just have paid to get there.

Secondary school had been rough on Clip. He was a small guy that made excellent grades without trying. It would have been worse if Harmon hadn't let everyone know that Clip was his brother. They lived in the same foster center, so it was mostly true. The first day of school, Harmon had laid down the law—if you messed with Clip, you messed up.

At the age of fourteen, he beat three seniors senseless for attempting to put Clip in a trash container. One of them was a Yalteen, a member of a race of large humanoids from two systems over. It wasn't a fair fight—they should have brought more people with them. Harmon hated bullies.

137

After the suspension ended, the school's Warball coach came to see him. He started that season as a freshman and worked on using it to earn a scholarship to the academy. By the time he graduated, he was six feet two inches with two hundred and twenty pounds of muscle. He got the scholarship and a shot at going into space. It was the longest time he'd ever spent away from his foster brother, but he couldn't turn it down.

Clip stayed on Joth and went to work for Rinto. He figured it was a job that would get him access to all kinds of technical stuff, servos, motors, and maybe even some alien computers. The first week he was there, he tweaked the equipment and increased the plant's recycled steel production by 12 percent. Rinto was eternally grateful, as it put him solidly into the profit column instead of toeing the line between profit and loss. When Harmon came back to the planet after the academy, Rinto hired him on the spot on Clip's recommendation. After he saw Harmon operate the grappler and got to know him, he was glad he did.

A steady beeping brought Harmon back to the present. Clip's program had succeeded in unlocking the container. "Right on!" Clip exclaimed. He was always using expressions hundreds or more years out of style. "Let's see what we have; I hope this one isn't empty, too." Last month they'd come across a smaller vault, but it had been empty.

Harmon stepped up and wedged his hands into the small opening the door had made when it disengaged the locks. There wasn't enough power in the small cells Clip used to open it any further. He put his weight into it, and the door opened enough for them to get inside. Before they went in, Harmon placed a piece of pipe in the doorway so it couldn't close and lock on them, baking them alive before anyone realized they were missing.

Daylight shone in through the doorway, and they both froze in place; the weapons vault was full.

\* \* \* \* \*

Get "Salvage Title" now at:
https://www.amazon.com/dp/B07H8Q3HBV.

Find out more about Kevin Steverson and "Salvage Title" at:
http://chriskennedypublishing.com/.

\* \* \* \* \*

The following is an
**Excerpt from Book One of The Progenitors' War:**

# A Gulf in Time

---

# Chris Kennedy

Available from Theogony Books

eBook, Paperback, and (Soon) Audio

**Excerpt from "A Gulf in Time:"**

"Thank you for calling us," the figure on the front view screen said, his pupil-less eyes glowing bright yellow beneath his eight-inch horns. Generally humanoid, the creature was blood red and had a mouthful of pointed teeth that were visible when he smiled. Giant bat wings alternately spread and folded behind him; his pointed tail could be seen flicking back and forth when the wings were folded. "We accept your offer to be our slaves for now and all eternity."

"Get us out of here, helm!" Captain Sheppard ordered. "Flank speed to the stargate!"

"Sorry, sir, my console is dead," the helmsman replied.

"Can you jump us to the Jinn Universe?"

"No, sir, that's dead too."

"Engineer, do we have our shields?"

"No, sir, they're down, and my console's dead, too."

"OSO? DSO? Status?"

"My console's dead," the Offensive Systems Officer replied.

"Mine, too," the Defensive Systems Officer noted.

The figure on the view screen laughed. "I do *so* love the way new minions scamper about, trying to avoid the unavoidable."

"There's been a mistake," Captain Sheppard said. "We didn't intend to call you or become your minions."

"It does not matter whether you *intended* to or not," the creature said. "You passed the test and are obviously strong enough to function as our messengers."

"What do you mean, 'to function as your messengers?'"

"It is past time for this galaxy's harvest. You will go to all the civilizations and prepare them for the cull."

"I'm not sure I like the sound of that. What is this 'cull?'"

"We require your life force in order to survive. Each civilization will be required to provide 98.2% of its life force. The remaining 1.8% will be used to reseed their planets."

"And you expect us to take this message to all the civilized planets in this galaxy?"

"That is correct. Why else would we have left the stargates for you to use to travel between the stars?"

"What if a civilization doesn't want to participate in this cull?"

"Then they will be obliterated. Most will choose to save 1.8% of their population, rather than none, especially once you make an example or two of the civilizations who refuse."

"And if *we* refuse?"

"Then your society will be the first example."

"I can't make this kind of decision," Captain Sheppard said, stalling. "I'll have to discuss it with my superiors."

"Unacceptable. You must give me an answer now. Kneel before us or perish; those are your choices."

"I can't," Captain Sheppard said, his voice full of anguish.

"Who called us by completing the quest?" the creature asked. "That person must decide."

"I pushed the button," Lieutenant Commander Hobbs replied, "but I can't commit my race to this any more than Captain Sheppard can."

"That is all right," the creature said. "Sometimes it is best to have an example from the start." He looked off screen. "Destroy them."

"Captain Sheppard, there are energy weapons warming up on the other ship," Steropes said.

"DSO, now would be a good time for those shields..." Captain Sheppard said.

"I'm sorry, sir; my console is still dead."

"They're firing!" Steropes called.

The enemy ship fired, but the *Vella Gulf*'s shields snapped on, absorbing the volley.

"Nice job, DSO!" Captain Sheppard exclaimed.

"I didn't do it, sir!" the DSO cried. "They just came on."

"Well, if you didn't do it, who did?" Captain Sheppard asked.

"I don't know!" the DSO exclaimed. "All I know is we can't take another volley like that, sir; the first round completely maxed out our shields. One more, and they're going to fail!"

"I...activated...the shields," Solomon, the ship's artificial intelligence, said. The voice of the AI sounded strained. "Am fighting...intruder..." the AI's voice fluctuated between male and female. "Losing...system...integrity...krelbet gelched."

"Krelbet gelched?" the DSO asked.

"It means 'systems failing' in the language of the Eldive," Steropes said.

"The enemy is firing again," the DSO said. "We're hit! Shields are down."

"I've got hits down the length of the ship," the duty engineer said. "We're open to space in several places. We can't take another round like that!"

"That was just the little that came through after the shields fell," the DSO said. "We're doomed if—*missiles inbound!* I've got over 100 missiles inbound, and I can't do anything to stop them!" He switched to the public address system. "*Numerous missiles inbound! All hands brace for shock! Five seconds! Three...two...one...*"

\* \* \* \* \*

Get "A Gulf in Time" now at:
https://www.amazon.com/dp/B0829FLV92

Find out more about Chris Kennedy and "A Gulf in Time" at:
https://chriskennedypublishing.com/imprints-authors/chris-kennedy/

\* \* \* \* \*

Made in the USA
Coppell, TX
22 April 2021